'Unpin your hair,' he ordered, and relieved her of the pretty yellow satin flowers. 'But, before you do, take another sip of the wine.'

She unpinned her hair and let it fall like a shiny dark fountain covering her shoulders. She shivered, and took a fresh sip of the wine. It burned, but not nearly so much as his hands burned through the silk of her dress. He was caressing her now. His hands running through her hair, over her shoulders, down to her neat little breasts. She gasped, but was incapable of doing anything except stare like a hypnotised fawn into the dramatic blackness of his eyes.

'You are mine,' he told her. 'To do with as I will. You belong to me, Sea Jade, and you will do as I say . . .'

Irene Roberts lives with her husband, well-known local artist, Trevor Roberts, in Malborough village, South Devon. She has two sons, one daughter, three cats and three dogs. After due consideration Irene believes that the three cats are the bosses of her home.

Irene Roberts has written over 100 novels under her own name and various pseudonyms. She has been featured on local television programmes and has often been a guest on Devon radio, BBC and Devonair. She is Founder Life President of Kingsbridge Writers and is Reviews Editor of the South Hams Newspaper group.

She has written two other Masquerade Historical Romances, *Moonpearl* and *Kingdom of the Sun*.

SEA JADE

Irene Roberts

MILLS & BOON LIMITED
ETON HOUSE   18–24 PARADISE ROAD
RICHMOND   SURREY   TW9 1SR

First published in Great Britain 1987 by Mills & Boon Limited

© Irene Roberts 1987

Australian copyright 1987 Philippine copyright 1987

ISBN 0 263 75805 2

Set in 10 on 10½ pt Linotron Times 04–0887–76,200

Photoset by Rowland Phototypesetting Limited Bury St Edmunds, Suffolk Made and printed in Great Britain by Cox and Wyman Limited, Reading

CHAPTER ONE

It was the Hour of the Dragon, the great triumphant beast who came sailing benevolently over the misty mountains with wings outspread. It was Dragon who greeted the sun as his equal and who personally ushered in the light of each new day.

Early though Dragon was, the ladies of the Ling household were already sipping tea and nibbling honeyed locust-dates in the courtyard of their home. Lilting laughter curled upwards as airily as the smoke from Peach Velvet's cigarette. The object of Number One Lady's teasing was, as usual, the slight, infinitely lovely, Sea Jade. The girl, now seventeen years old, had been adopted into the family when a very young child.

'*Ha!*' Peach Velvet pointed her long ebony cigarette-holder in Sea Jade's direction. 'I tell you, there is no mystery about our lord's visit to Tientsin this time! A little imp told me that the moment has come for special arrangements to be made for you.'

The wives and concubines began laughing, high and sweet, and teasing Sea Jade, whom they loved, and she laughed back at them, wrinkling her nose. Her world was one of silken gowns, embroidered slippers, lanterns and paper fans. Her days were filled to overflowing with such interesting things as discussions of make-up, board-games, gossiping, and eating little kumquat oranges the size of plums. Of course, there were the walks one took, to give pleasure to the lustily singing caged birds one held. Then there was Moon Gate time, wonder time, when one stood very still and just listened to the music God's breath made as he blew against the windbells hanging so prettily in the acacia trees.

Sea Jade fluttered her paper fan. It was decorated with lotus flowers a shade deeper than the rose-coloured tunic she wore.

'I cannot bear the thought of special arrangements,' she cried in mock alarm. 'Besides, who would want own humble self?'

'I cannot think,' Peach Velvet replied, and nodded her head, her eyes twinkling in the loveliness of her lined face. 'But I am sure of this. Your husband will be as ideal as has always been promised. He will be a student; a very upright, honest and academic man. He will be a deeply thinking lord who will satisfy even your flighty little soul.'

'Is not her soul that must be satisfied!' Small Plum, one of the concubines, joked. 'Can think of things, nothing to do with mind, that new lord should do to please pretty young wife.'

At this, the laughter and joking rose like a wave of joy and mischievousness in the air. Fragile hands clapped together, fans fluttered, and Sea Jade's protestations were drowned as the teasing reached fresh heights.

Suddenly a serving-girl rushed in. Her face bore a look of permanent surprise, since her pigtailed hair was pulled back so tightly. But now her eyes were afraid, her manner agitated.

Not waiting for ceremony, she cried out, 'Missee Sea Jade, Missee Sea Jade, a message! A message direct from Empress. See? Here is scroll bearing the August One's seal.'

'What is this?' the ladies cried, their laughter banished. 'Are you mad?'

'The messenger gave me this,' the girl insisted. 'He say that her Imperial Majesty will grant Missee Sea Jade audience in Winter Palace. A royal litter will be sent within the hour.'

Sea Jade looked down at the scroll that bore the royal seal. She was suddenly terrified, confused, completely taken aback.

'The August, the Imperial T'zu Hsi?' she whispered. 'She has sent for own worthless self?'

'Within the hour?' the ladies wailed.

'Towels, water, scent, chop-chop!' Peach Velvet commanded briskly. 'There is much to do.'

'Wear blue,' Small Plum suggested. 'Is like summer sky, very good, very pretty.'

'No, green. Palest green – like leaves of bamboo.'

'Red as a bridal dress. Red is colour of good luck.'

'No. Colour of sunshine . . .'

Dazed, Sea Jade allowed them to fuss and fret around her like so many nervous linnets. They adored her and she them, but they all knew that they were helpless. Why, oh why, was the honourable Ling Fu so long away? He would know what to do, how to advise! But he was on one of his city visits again. With friends—but he never said who they were. It had not mattered . . . till now.

Much too quickly there came the high-pitched screeching and shouting from the servants outside. The litter, curtained with royal yellow, had arrived. Sea Jade went to it and entered, her calm expression belying the nerves clawing at her inside. She was beautiful in peach silk, and hairpins decorated with little pink pearl tassels quivered like rosy raindrops on her dark topknot of hair.

The men bearing the litter on long shoulder-poles set off at a steady rhythmic pace. Sea Jade was borne through a network of streets and squares crowded with people of all races and creeds. Beyond this, bounding the northern edge of the square, was Tienanmen Gate, entrance to the Forbidden City, heart of the Empire and the Universe, where Imperial decrees were read out. Enormous double doors studded with bronze were swung back at the litter-bearers' cry, and Sea Jade's heart began to beat too quickly, with excitement and fear. They passed along avenues of cherry trees and saw beautiful houses with conical roofs and golden yellow tiles. There was a building shaped like a series of coolies' hats piled one above another, gardens where grew willow trees, bamboo, and the mountain rhododendrons that would soon turn the world into a fairyland of pink and purple and mauve-blue. On they went, along passages open to the sky that were interrupted every so often with red-laquered doors with gilt dragon designs. Clouds of white doves were flying free, and the tinkling, mysterious music of crystal windbells whispered against Sea Jade's ears. She was also conscious of the aroma of moxa incense heavy in the air.

The litter was set down, and a man wearing a flamboyant robe of kingfisher blue embroidered with a green and gold peacock came to meet her. He helped her to alight and indicated that she must follow him. She drew in a deep breath, smoothed her long, slim-fitting dress, and walked down a short corridor. Its end was blocked by enormously tall and elegant red doors, again emblazoned with massive golden dragons, which opened silently at their approach.

Dazed, hardly able to believe that she was in the Forbidden City, Sea Jade was at first hardly able to take in the sheer opulence of the scene. The walls were hung with curtains of yellow silk. There were white chairs, beautifully carved and with velvet seats, cabinets lacquered in black and gold, exquisite Ming vases and other artefacts of gold and silver, jade and jet, and ornaments studded with precious stones. Great carved screens were inlaid with lapis lazuli, silver, ivory and gold. Gods and goddesses stood implacably in flower-bedecked shrines, and she saw statues of holy animals with ruby red eyes and snarling ivory teeth.

Then Sea Jade froze. Ahead, at the far end of the sumptuous royal hall, stood a dais. On this, on a tremendous throne, sat her Imperial Majesty. Below the dais, a semi-circle of officials dressed in splendid robes were standing with their hands folded inside their wide sleeves. Those of royal blood wore the Imperial yellow. They were gods but, Sea Jade thought, they looked like wooden dolls, and she wanted to die.

Yehonola, T'zu Hsi, Empress Dowager and effective ruler of China for over forty years, looked down at the girl who was now, as instructed, prostrate full length on the floor, her head buried in her arms. The old woman's eyes were black, hooded like a lizard's, and as empty. All facial expression was held in tight control by her mask of enamel make-up. She wore an elaborate head-dress of tassels, flowers and gems on her carefully coif-fured shiny hair. Her dress, of finest silk, was long and intricately designed. Multicoloured bands of china beads and silk edged the lower hem and also the wide sleeves. Her slender hands flashed with many jewels. Her elongated nail-sheaths were encrusted with gems, and each of her two little fingers stretched to five inches or more. The silence and waiting were unbearable, and Sea Jade's heart was refusing to slow down. With all her soul she was wishing that Ling Fu were there to help her, or that her mother had let her die, and not sold her all those years ago. From a long way away she heard at last the high, clear, porcelain-hard sound of Yehonola Empress Dowager's voice.

'We are pleased that you are here to carry out Im-perial duties, Miss Ling. You will follow explicit orders of court. You will do as you are told joyfully, and the birds of heaven will convey loving messages direct to your ancestors.'

Sea Jade dared neither to move nor to reply.

'We understand that you have been educated in the English tongue.' There was a faint impatience and con-tempt in her Imperial Majesty's tone, and she went on. 'Your honourable lord father is known to us as a brilliant and intellectual personage whom we hold in high esteem. Should you please us, we shall see to it that high privileges are showered upon him and all members of his house.' There was a significant pause, then the Empress continued, 'It is our wish that you be taken to Mission House of Golden Lilies, and there become member of that establishment. The missionary, a Mr Morrow, works for the British officials as interpreter. He will be one of the first to know the delivery date of fresh English arms supplies. It will be auspicious for us to know the exact time and place of the arrival of the barbarian guns. We plan that you will be a resident in the mission. There you will listen and learn . . . then impart everything you hear to us.'

Sea Jade remained frozen, and looked like a fallen peach blossom clinging to the ground. I am to be used as a spy! she thought, and felt sick with horror at the idea.

The Empress continued, 'To gain the trust of the missionaries, you will appear to have helped one of their kind. It will seem that you have gone to the rescue of a certain Mr Paul Aubrey, who is to be the new helper there. How this is to be achieved will be explained to you later. We know that you will follow instructions with correctness and care. If you do not . . .'

The voice became metallic, and Sea Jade knew exactly what would happen to her beloved lord father, and all the members of his house, if she did not do exactly as she was told. Then she was dismissed from the royal presence.

'Must wait for instructor,' a manservant told her. 'Go to side room; be patient. Take care!'

Sea Jade waited, out of sight of the main corridor. Then she heard the hushed rustling movements of many feet; clearly, someone of great importance was approaching. From behind her protecting screen, she peeped out, to see a tall, dark, very regal-looking man in mandarin's clothes walking purposefully towards the great doors of the Audience Hall. His long tunic was blue, with, on the front, the large gold emblem bearing the crest of Han. The ceremonial hat with a peacock feather perched jauntily on the back of his head. His hair was tied away from his face, gathered in a short queue. He was handsome and arrogant. Even at that first startled glance, Sea Jade recognised that here was a man who would never cringe before the old woman who so closely gripped China in her greedy hands. He would show courtesy, yes, but he would bear himself with dignity and pride at all times. She found herself wanting very much to witness the meeting between this striking man and the Dowager Empress.

The woman on the throne raised one brow to signify that she would hold further audience. Uniformed guards swung back the doors, and the Lord Han Shen strode through. He walked forward, a man's man, and upon reaching the correct position, sank to the ground with great dignity and touched his forehead three times on the tiled floor. Then he waited, but there was something of a coiled-spring look about the magnificent figure whose actions were so carefully correct.

'My honourable Lord Han,' the Dowager Empress said, 'it is to be your duty to watch over and protect an ignorant peasant girl who will shortly find herself on your land.'

Han Shen's back stiffened. Such a menial task was beneath his contempt, but he dared make no reply. He could almost feel the stabbing glance directed against the back of his neck.

'The girl is of some small significance to us,' the Empress went on, and there was now a black silk menace in her tone. 'You will therefore do your duty without question, Han Shen. Now you may go. Lord Ho Chei will explain our wishes more fully to you. He waits in our offices outside.'

Han Shen made his obeisances again, and, having been given permission to rise, made his way, backwards, towards the door. He was not aware of Sea Jade. He was conscious only of the cold anger in his soul.

Sea Jade was not allowed to go home. Her fine clothes and jewels were taken from her, and she was dressed in a coarse cotton tunic and trousers of blue. They allowed her to keep the flute she carried with her everywhere, and also gave her a string of copper coins to be used in an emergency.

The plan was simplicity itself. She had to wait near the Iris Pool until Paul Aubrey came by. He would be waylaid, and she would rescue him. From then on, she must make the journey to the mission take as long as possible—and her own lowly self indispensable. She must become close and infinitely dear to the white foreign devil. So much so, that by the time they arrived at their destination, he would automatically keep her with him and never even think of letting her go.

'You will go to extraordinary lengths to ensnare the man's admiration,' the cold-looking, very superior, official told her. 'Do I make myself clear?'

She shook her head in a miserable affirmation.

'You have memorised exactly where Mission House of Golden Lilies is situated, and the roundabout route you must take?'

'Yes,' she whispered.

'Good. You will not be alone. You may think you are, but that will not be the case. You will have help if it is necessary. However, it is to be hoped that you will manage to perform important duty alone. Now, do you understand exactly what you must do?'

'Yes.'

The following evening Sea Jade was escorted outside the city to a country place called the Iris Pool. The men who had accompanied the bullock cart in which she had travelled then disappeared from view, but she was aware that they were hiding near. She looked up at the sky, knowing that the great Yellow River was so long that it finally joined the Milky Way and became the River of Stars. The two celestial waterways united in a circle above and below the earth to embrace the whole of mankind lovingly. Nervously she slipped her flute from inside her sleeve and began to play a soft, hauntingly beautiful tune of old China. At a warning hiss from the rock behind her, she froze. A few minutes later came the sound of hoofs and human voices. She slipped the flute back inside her sleeve as two men came into view. Clear in the moonlight she saw an old Chinaman and a young barbarian, who had light hair and was dressed like a Chinese.

'Have feeling this is bad joss place,' the old man said urgently.

'Worse than a mile or so back – and the other hassle outside the railway? I thought we were done for there, Li. It was good of you to come to meet me.'

Suddenly there came a fanatical yelling, and men leapt out of the shadows. Claw-like hands reached up and pulled the men off their mounts. Horrified, Sea Jade watched as the white barbarian fought back, but he received a tremendous blow from a staff. Still struggling, game to the last, he fought on, but a further blow knocked him senseless to the ground. The old China-man, too, was putting up a fierce struggle, when there came a terrible sound like the roar of a dragon, and a third figure sprang upon the scene: a giant black and tan wolfhound, such a beast as Sea Jade had never seen before. So great was the ferocity of the huge animal that the fanatics gave cries of terror and ran.

The old Chinaman, having given one last despairing look at the fallen white man, ran after the avenging dog. Weeping silently, Sea Jade remained hidden. She watched and waited all night long, almost too afraid to breathe. Neither Chinaman nor dog returned, and the wicked men, even those who were supposedly there to guard her own humble self, had seemed to vanish into thin air. Then a miracle occurred: the barbarian moved, and groaned. He had not been killed, after all!

It took a great deal of courage for Sea Jade to creep nearer to him. The breath caught in her throat in a gasp and her hand flew to her mouth. The man was large, and his hair, the colour of the mid-morning sun, was matted with blood. There was blood in his ear, and it was only too clear that he was desperately ill. In his face, empty of colour, his nose was strong she saw, and it jutted out in a most un-Chinese-like way. Yet, there was something about him that drew her.

Her hand fluttered to rest as gently as a butterfly against the masculine cheek. It was clammy. She continued to examine him, and sighed with relief to discover a pulse beating in his throat. Even so, all movement and consciousness seemed to have left him again. She ran to the pool, took a handful of leaves, and dipped them into the water until they were soaked. Returning to the barbarian, she gently dampened and wiped his face. After that, she sat beside him and waited, but she was mortally afraid. The attackers had not acted as had been planned, she was sure. They must have had loyalties to the Boxers rather than to the Imperial army. If that were the case, they might come back to finish off the white man – and to end her life, too. Even more horrifying, that awful black and yellow dog might come back, and—and he might eat her alive! The thought made her shiver anew.

Why had she not been told about the dog? Why had they not at least warned her of the proposed attack? All that she had been told with certainty was that she was to wait while the barbarian was waylaid. She was to make herself known to him, help him, and from then on stick to him like glue.

She thought back to the court official who had instructed her. How polite he had been, how godly and austere. Yet, all the time, he must have known that the barbarian was to be ambushed in a cruel and ruthless way. She, Sea Jade, officially adopted into the honourable House of Ling Fu, had not been considered worthy enough to be told the truth! With all her heart she wished that Ling Fu was near.

Sea Jade bit her lip and wondered wildly what the August Father would think about all this. He liked English people, and respected them even though he did not go along with everything they said. He had been close to Mary and Martin Fairbrother, English missionaries in Tientsin. It was they who had heard of a high-born lady who had run away because she had been ordered to smother her unwanted girl-child. Starving, and near to death, the frantic young mother had sold Sea Jade to them for threepence.

Sea Jade's feet had never been bound, and she was brought up as a young lady. When the Fairbrothers had died within days of each other from a particularly virulent fever, Ling Fu had stepped in. For the sake of his English friends, he said, he would take care of Sea Jade. He decided that she should become a daughter of his own and take the name of Ling. Once, he himself had had a daughter, but Silver Dove had been married a long time ago. A bride, sadly, was no longer considered to be part of her father's house. After that, Sea Jade took the place of the daughter Ling Fu had loved and lost because she now lived so very far away. On a small island, he had said, off the main coast.

Two tears slipped silently down Sea Jade's cheeks. Her revered adoptive father, with his inch-long nails and beautiful long thin face with its fine wispy white beard, was the light of her life. For him, she would do all that they ordered. If it were necessary, she would lie and cheat and steal – but how she wished there could have been a kinder, more subtle, way! Those men, those wicked, treacherous men, were killers. The others, supposedly her guards and protectors, were long gone. There was nothing she could do now except wait.

She busied herself by collecting scrub and branches and building them into a shelter of sorts for the unconscious man. When he suddenly began to speak, the sound of his voice made her jump.

'Yes, sir, you're right . . . Always right! Sir, I do have thoughts, ideas, concepts entirely my own . . . Yes, sir, will do as you say . . . Always have, always will, but . . . Oh, dear God, perhaps . . .' As he gabbled, Sea Jade's heart went out to him.

After a while, not knowing quite what to do, she decided to stretch her legs, and walked along the path the Chinaman had taken. She came upon the old man's corpse, and her hands flew to her mouth to stop the high scream that leapt to her throat. It had not been necessary to kill the old man, she grieved. It was horrible, wicked, obscene! Not too far away she saw the still, battered body of the dog.

Suddenly fear of the loneliness, of unseen spirits and ancestors that she was sure must be hovering about the place, made her turn on her heel and run back to the barbarian. He looked as though he had not moved all the time she had been away. All that day she sat there, returning every so often to the Iris Pool for water. With this, she dampened the pale lips and strangely handsome foreign face. She felt at one with him—on his side.

Clouds glowed red and gold as the sky flared a bloody defiance of darkness. But, clad in his indigo slippers, Night was already creeping in at the east. Mottled shadows now stretched like ink-blots from the bases of rocks and shrubs. Hawks wheeled above in casually intricate flight before finally returning to roost.

A thin sickle of moon was slicing the black and silver scud high above the hills when Paul Aubrey regained consciousness. The pale light it threw down silvered the fairness of his hair. His pale skin gleamed, and Sea Jade saw that his eyes were blue. For a long time he stared at her, then, as she gently brushed a lock of hair away from his forehead, his mouth trembled in the beginning of a smile. A large sensitive hand reached out to touch her face, almost as though he was trying to make sure that she was real. His touch was one of gentle gratitude. Sea Jade was surprised at the rush of protective emotion that raged through her. It was all too clear that here was no white devil who skinned and ate Chinese children—as was universally believed. Here was no ogre who fed on Chinese souls! Here was a white barbarian, admittedly, but one her own father would welcome into his house.

In a vague way, Paul was conscious of the beautiful girl whom he still half believed to be a figment of a dream. But, then, nothing seemed real. There was an agony in his head and a numbness in his mind. He tried to clutch at reason, and found himself conscious only of the excruciating pain.

Sea Jade asked quietly, 'Is honourable lord all better now?'

In spite of his condition, he thought the girl's high sweet voice sounded like a harp drenched in sunlight, and his sense of unreality persisted rather than the reverse. He tried to sit up, but the agony increased, and he felt nausea. Small hands were pushing firmly against his chest.

'Is good to stay still. Is correct. Honourable lord, he must take plenty time now.'

A sound came from behind them, and she froze. It came again, and she turned, half expecting to see a terrible spirit, or the dead Chinaman's ghost. Two fiery eyes were glittering lights against the blackness. There was a harsh panting sound of an animal in distress, and an occasional faint whine. Slowly the great dog crawled forwards on his belly. Clearly he was in deep pain. Ignoring Sea Jade's slight, tense figure, he managed to reach Paul. Then he rested his lathered, weary head on his master's chest, and stayed still.

'Rayn!' Paul croaked. 'Good—good boy. Good ol' boy!'

'Is hurt,' Sea Jade whispered hesitantly. 'Is hurt bad.'

'Please—please see what you can do for him.' There was a wealth of feeling in Paul's voice. 'I—I don't seem to be able to move.'

'Needs water, needs rest,' Sea Jade told him, then, for the man's sake, she added with a confidence she did not feel, 'Will be all right.'

Like a wraith in the moonlight, she slipped away from man and dog and went to the Iris Pool for water. She did what she could for both of them. When the night grew cold, Paul began to shiver. His eyes were closed, and he began calling for Shane and talking to someone he called 'Sir'. Sea Jade crept close, so that her body warmth reached out to enfold him. Eventually they were all asleep while the River of Stars flowed on endlessly in the heavens that, at the right and proper time, would give way to the morning sun.

The fresh new dawn was taking silver footsteps into the day when Sea Jade looked shyly into the barbarian's face. He had taken a drink of cold water and seemed a littte better, but his eyes were dazed. The wound he had received was very bad; nothing could disguise that. Her heart went out to him.

'What you name?' she asked shyly.

Paul, still feeling unreal and sick because the agony in his head seemed to have increased, brushed his hand across his eyes. He tried to concentrate. For the girl, he must! She was exquisite. Her large almond-shaped eyes glowed with care and compassion. Her skin was as fine as porcelain. Her hair was a shining waterfall dropping to her waist. She was tiny, fragile, and as she went to and fro from the pool she seemed to glide, for all her feet were unbound. Perhaps she is Manchu, he thought vaguely; she is not a peasant, I'm sure. But the thought wafted away into the mist until her high sweet voice brought him back again.

'What you name?' she asked again, and tilted her head to one side as enquiringly as an inquisitive bird.

'I—I am Paul,' he said hoarsely, and found speaking a great effort. 'Paul Aubrey.'

'All very good and correct name. I am Sea Jade.'

'Very—very pretty,' he said, and wondered why his voice sounded so tinny and far away. 'You—you should not be out here . . . alone.'

'Alone all the time,' she told him, remembering the part she had to play. 'Alone since old enough to look after own lowly self.'

'You speak English very—very well.'

'Missionary! Chinese Christian Mission House,' she said truthfully. 'In Tientsin, all long time ago.'

'I—I served at Tientsin!' He brushed a shaking hand across his eyes. 'But was sent . . . Think I had to get to . . . There was something—someone.' He started up, then gasped and grimaced with pain. 'Li! I . . . There was a man with me, a Chinese named Li. We were going to the Golden Lilies Mission, and . . . Oh God,' his voice faded almost to a whisper, 'why is it that nothing seems clear?'

'Bad mens came, lord. Hit you on head.'

'Thieves?'

'All same not thieves.'

'Fanatics,' he said, and whispered wearily, 'Oh Lord, I should have guessed. Probably Boxers. They—they are killing missionaries and converts like flies. Thought it was all up with us way back, but—but the Imperial troops stepped in and helped.' He groaned then. 'Oh Lord, it's all such a muddle. I feel as if there's a steamroller crushing over my head. Could—could you ask Li to come here, please, and—and where's old Rayn? Not right without him around. I say . . .'

He sank down again and closed his eyes.

Sea Jade explained, 'Wicked mens come and knock you all down. China friend and dog runned after them. Dog here now, you not remember he here? China friend he not here. He went after wicked mens.'

'The brave old fool! I must go after him. I must . . .'

'Same like last time,' she told him. 'You not understand. You not strong enough yet. Not auspicious to move.'

'But Li, my friend . . .'

'Chinaman, he have bad joss. He finish.'

'Finish?' He was puzzled and trying hard to hold on to reason. 'What do you mean, finish?'

'He die. He all dead. You not talk any more. Must rest.'

He stared at her as memory began to return. They had

warned that there might be trouble, but news from the Mission House of the Golden Lilies had been bad. James Morrow was very ill, fatally so. He needed all the help and comfort to be had. Li, Morrow's right-hand man, showing up when he had clinched it. They had taken a sampan from Tientsin to the dock and railway at Yang-tsun. The train had proceeded across the plain for some sixty miles to reach the junction town of Feng-tai. Here the railroad forked, one arm swinging left towards Hankow and the Yangtze, the other right, to Peking itself. But there had been rumours that the Peking line was blocked. The Chinese hated the railway. It carried fiery monsters on its back: monsters who rudely awakened the Spirits of the Earth. Paul and Li had decided to make the rest of the journey by horse. They had run into a mob just outside Feng-tai, but Imperial troops had dispersed the crowd. Everything had gone smoothly from then on, until now . . .

His mouth was dry as he asked, 'How—how do you know about Li?'

'Went look-see. Went this way, that way. I find. He all gone. Bad mens finish all same they think finish dog.' She raised two beautifully arched brows. 'Sea Jade take Chinese friend's place. You mind?'

'I—I must find him.' He was clearly fighting to keep conscious. 'There—there are certain things that must be done for him.

'Is happy with ancestors now,' she pointed out. 'You say prayers for China friend here.'

'Help—me—to him, I beg of you.'

Sea Jade motioned towards the dog. 'If mans move, dog will try follow. Then dog, he die. Be all finish like China friend.'

'Poor old Rayn,' Paul whispered. 'Poor ol' boy.' His hand moved slowly over the sleek brown and yellow head. Rayn opened his eyes, and the tip of his tail gave the merest quiver.

'Is getting all right,' Sea Jade pointed out. 'Must stay

here, get strong. Chinaman, he gone away to Other Country. Is happy with honourable ancestors. Nothing you do or say can help him now.'

'But, don't you understand . . .' His voice was weakening again. 'I really—really ought to try . . .'

'Dog, he bleed and die,' Sea Jade insisted in her gentle way.

'Oh Lord!' Paul gasped. 'I don't think I'd make it, anyway. There's something wrong. I'm as weak as a kitten, and there's this terrible pain and throbbing in my head.'

'Will get more drink,' she told him, and her lips curved upwards at the edges in a faint smile. 'Belly not empty when filled with water. Water come from holy mountain. Is sweet. Is good!'

She left the man and the pathetically weak animal and went to the Iris Pool. She was shaking inside and mortally afraid. The plan had gone terribly wrong: she had been left here with neither help nor food, yet she was supposed to keep this man alive and safe. And it could not have been planned—what had happened to the barbarian's China friend. No, she would never believe that! The barbarian must never know the truth. It was unacceptable to her that her own people had committed this horrendous act.

Although she tried to forget the sight she had seen, the macabre spectre danced in her mind, making her want to scream. Li's naked body had been skewered out over a rock. He had been terribly mutilated and cut about. His face was contorted, his dead eyes glassy and glaring. His mouth was pulled back in a grimace of agony, yet it had come over almost as an evil kind of grin. There had been a bloodstained note actually pinned to the bony chest with a sliver of bamboo. It read: 'Filthy Rice Christian. Rot in seven hells. Die as all will die.'

Sea Jade was a 'Rice Christian', as were all Chinese who believed in the English God, or even liked the people with white faces, colourless eyes and long noses.

If the men came back, she knew they would kill her, whether she was on orders from the Empress or not. Yes, they would kill her—after a time. The barbarian would be slaughtered where he lay. They would, of course, eat the dog.

Panic-stricken, Sea Jade wondered whether the illustrious Ling Fu had returned from Tientsin, and whether he had any idea of what was happening to her. If only she could get a message to him, perhaps he would help. She needed help. The barbarian was too weak to move. Sea Jade began praying to *Yesu*, the English God, but for good measure she also sent her entreaties to China's most powerful god of all, the great and omnipotent August Personage of Jade. But no answer was forthcoming. She had to get man and dog to a better hiding-place. Her instructions had been to take the barbarian to an inn a half-*li* away. But he was too large for her to move, and quite incapable of helping himself at this stage. She returned to Paul and Rayn, and carefully squeezed water into their mouths.

'Thank you,' Paul gasped, and felt the world spinning in a crazy way because of the incessant beating and pounding in his head. A pounding that was shot through every so often by lightning strikes of pain. He reached out blindly, and took Sea Jade's hand.

'Is bad joss to stay!' Sea Jade's voice held all of the weary uncertainty in the world. 'Bad joss to move. I not know what to do. Wicked mens might come back. Might finish us.' Two feverish blue eyes were looking at her.

In a vague way, Paul knew that this beautiful girl was trying to help him. Knew that she was bewildered and afraid. Because she did not know what to do, he must try to pull his wits about him and help her. His mind slipped away, leaving only the knowledge that for the moment, at least, he was as helpless as she. He was capable only of lying still to try to beat the agony that seemed to be ripping his head in half. From a long way away he heard her voice. It was soft, gentle, whispering like gossamer through the waves of pain.

'Mission House too far,' she was saying. 'But know of good joss place. Called Inn of Great Security and Content. Not mind barbarians there. Must go there when auspicious moment comes. We call on gods and try—now?'

She was kneeling beside him, trying to lift him, and he attempted to meet her half way and help himself. It was no use. He moaned, and fell back into unconsciousness. Sea Jade squatted next to him, her strength gone. She felt useless and deathly afraid, but knew that she must not show it, must not lose face! She must remember at all times that she was a member of the honourable House of Ling. She began thinking wistfully of the meals at home. Of the great central bowl of steaming rice, the little dishes of cubed meat and fish, the bowls of soup, marzipan shapes and sunflower seeds.

Time passed slowly. The barbarian looked lifeless and his lips had gone blue. The dog whimpered every so often, but he stayed still, his long, pointed face laid lovingly against the chest of his master.

The weather changed. Light became harsh and clear. A cold wind scuffed up little devils of whirling dust. Sea Jade felt very alone, but when at last she heard the sound of someone approaching, her fear of isolation was lost in the terror of knowing that she would be discovered with a hated barbarian. She wanted to run and hide, but did not. She continued to squat by the man and his dog, and sent up frantic prayers to the gods.

Amazed, she found that she recognised the personage who came riding up on a magnificent black horse. He was accompanied by a troup of personal guards in uniforms of dark and light blue. On the backs of their tunics, embroidered in gold silk, were the emblems of the House of Han. The Lord Han Shen sat tall and dignified in the saddle. Bare-headed now, his black hair was pulled tightly back from his handsome face and held in position by a wide gold comb. His eyes were dark and piercing. In his belt was a sharp knife, and also a quiver with arrows. There was a bow held at the back of his knee-length red and gold tunic by a wide silk cord, over black trousers tucked into tall riding-boots.

He came up to Sea Jade, but ignored her, looking round at the barren loneliness, his face expressionless. Having dismounted, he stepped near to look down into Paul's white countenance, and then he turned to Sea Jade who, still on her knees, bowed low so that her forehead touched the ground. She kowtowed three times.

'What are you doing here?' Han Shen asked, and his tone was glacier cold, and as bleak.

She dared not look up, but answered, 'Lord, he was set upon. His friend killed, the dog hurt. I have . . .' Her voice almost faded away, but then dignity came to her aid. 'I have tried to help. That is all.'

'Why have you stayed alone with him in this god-forsaken place?'

'I could not leave him to—to die, lord.'

'He is known to you?' Black eyes flashed, and she had the strange feeling that this powerful man had examined her minutely from head to toe and found her wanting. 'How well is he known to you?'

'He is a stranger who needed help, lord. That is all.'

'Yet you have stayed with him. Why?'

She remembered her instructions, and again kowtowed low before replying, 'There was no one else, and I am alone.'

'You intend to look after him?'

'Yes.'

'How?'

'I must get him to the Inn of Great Security and Content.'

'Ah! The building stands inside the boundary of my land,' the nobleman said coldly. 'I am Han Shen.'

Immediately Sea Jade made obeisance again,

touching her forehead three times on the ground. Her heart was pounding and her mouth went dry. This lord, this aristocratic noble lord, could have her murdered on the spot if he so chose. She was a nothing, a no one. Worse, she was with a hated white devil, and she had dared to say that she wanted to get the barbarian to the shelter of a place built on his land! She waited, feeling sick, for the curt order and the blow to fall.

Instead, after a prolonged moment of silence, Han Shen said, 'I will see to it that you reach the Inn.'

He turned imperiously, without a further word, and they all rode away. Sea Jade knew that she must still wait.

Some time later, coolies trotted along the path that was narrow and rutted, and ragged with sharp stones. With much gesticulating and high querulous voices, they lifted Paul Aubrey on to a stretcher and began jogging off with him, having neither looked at nor shown any concern whatever about Sea Jade. Quietly determined, she began walking after them. Even though the dog whined sadly, she did not turn round, yet she felt the longing in the treacle-gold canine eyes.

The way became more populated, and all around was a buzz of activity. The air was thick with sounds: the rasp of a watermill, the plod of ploughing buffaloes, the creak of farm carts, the noise of people shouting to each other, arguing, bargaining, or just passing the time of the day. The road was bustling even more now, with baggage coolies laden with opium, rush-wicks, indigo and paper. The wildness had given way to fields that were already ablaze with the promise of crops, terraces stepping up the hills flaring yellow rape, grown for the oil. There were masses and ridges of new growth that would, quite soon, be covered with the dark purple-black of bean blossom. And above all, everywhere, was the exquisite grace of the bamboo. Sea Jade's breath caught harshly in her throat. Bamboo had fashioned the skewer that had pinned the bloody message to the chest of old Li—just under his cut scrawny throat.

They reached the mud wall of the Inn of Great
Security and Content, set apart from the village. Paul
Aubrey was carried through the gate that had swung
back silently at their approach. Clearly they were expected, and there would be no problems. Sea Jade sent
up a silent prayer of thanks to the gods for sending along
the noble Han Shen. Once inside the inn compound, she
saw that it had a foul mud-hole of a yard. Some men,
carters tending animals, looked at the stretcher and its
occupant with suspicion and loathing, but let it pass. Of
Sea Jade they took no notice at all. She saw the rubbish
dumped near the well, the sad-looking water-spirit in his
shrine, the utter dejection of the place.

She followed the coolies to the interior of the inn. Paul
was taken to a filthy room, where he was unceremoniously lifted off the stretcher and dumped on a
straw pallet on the floor. She bent over him, but he
seemed quite unaware of what was going on. She heard
the pigs grunting and scuffling in the sty next door and
the raucous caterwauling of carters high on rice wine,
who were in the room on the other side. There came a
noise behind her, and she swung round in fear.

It was the innkeeper, a small flat-faced man with
cunning eyes. He glared at her, gave a cursory glance at
the white man, then set down two bowls of curried rice.
In spite of all her pleading and coaxing, Paul was hardly
aware of the offering of food, let alone capable of eating
it. At last Sea Jade gave up, and squatting beside the
verminous pallet, she ate her fill.

That night, all was quiet in the inn, except for the
noises of pigs and the carters' snores. Paul was still; he
had been in fever and talking nonsense again, but now
he seemed to have fallen into a deep, natural sleep. His
face was white in the rushlight, but every so often he
called out for his dog. In spite of herself, Sea Jade found
that she, too, could not forget the look in the faithful
animal's eyes. If he had not been found, killed and eaten

already, she thought, there might be a chance. Very carefully she crept out of the inn and into the courtyard. The gate was closed. The gatekeeper, an old man with a cadaverous face, was asleep. As quietly as she could, she lifted the long wooden bar that secured the wide gate, and slipped outside. She began hurrying then, back along the path, towards where she had last seen Rayn.

She came upon him, lying exhausted by the stream that fed the watermill. He must have been inching his way along after them for a very long time. His fur was matted with dirt and sweat and blood.

'You come?' Sea Jade whispered gently. 'You come with us? Sea Jade see you all safe now. Sea Jade stay till your legs work all correct.' Then, mimicking the barbarian, 'Good boy. Good ol' boy!'

Rayn wearily lifted his head, and she reached out and stroked his face. He rested his lathered cheek against her knee and she was suddenly fiercely glad that she had come to find him. After a while, she managed to coax him to move. He was weak, his tail down, his tongue hung out, but he made his way alongside her, helped by the tiny hand curled round his wide studded collar. Once he looked up, right into her face, and Sea Jade found that she wanted to cry. She was wondering, with each step they took, if Paul, his dog and she would live long enough ever to reach the Mission House of the Golden Lilies.

She frowned, wondering about the white man who knew so many things to do with the English army. He must be very high up indeed if her Imperial Majesty knew of him and thought the messages he received were so important. What kind of Christian was he—to concern himself with things to do with the English army? No, that was not fair! He did nothing to help the army, merely acted as a translator. There was nothing wicked or underhand about that. And, besides, what did it matter? His mission house would at least be sweet and clean. And she had always found white Christians to be,

even though tremendously superior in attitude, very fair
and kind.

I pray to the gods, she thought, that I can reach the
honourable James Morrow in time! It came to her then
to marvel at how important the unknown missionary
was, in fact, to those she held dear. For the first time she
began to think seriously of and wonder about the unknown man who ran the Mission House of the Golden
Lilies. She tried to picture how he looked, how he spoke,
and she wondered just what he was doing at that
moment. James Morrow, she thought. He is called
Honourable James Morrow! Can he be as good and kind
as Fairweather Martin? Remembering two pairs of
loving blue eyes, the gentle touch of caring hands, made
her feel incredibly lonely and sad.

'Is no good.' She was forgetting to use the pidgin
English necessary for her part. 'I have lost my English
family,' she whispered. 'I am not like barbarians, I
am Chinese! I do this thing for the Empress, not for
barbarians. I not care if he all finish. If dog all finish.'

Rayn edged a little nearer to her, liking the faint
sound of her voice.

'Is all very proper,' she said softly to him, 'that you
know how greatly I lie. I do care, ol' boy! He is not finish,
you are not finish. We all not finish for a very long time!
We will get to Mr Morrow's mission all the same soon
now. He will help us, I know.'

'Father is gone. He is dead! He will work in this mission
no more. I cannot believe it—no, not even now!'

Christina Morrow's large blue eyes, fringed with
lashes as thick and as dark as her hair, were shadowed by
grief as she stood before the window of the mission that
was called House of the Golden Lilies. She was unaware
of the beautiful cut-out a distant pagoda made against
the early morning sky, nor was she conscious of the
tiled pavilions, the tea-house and the distant silver
shimmering of the wide canal.

She blinked. Grief so deep that she felt physically sick gripped and clawed at her stomach. She could not speak, dared not. She was vaguely conscious of Lotus standing close by her side. Christina turned to her blindly, then unable to meet the sorrow in her friend's almond-shaped eyes, she again continued to look through the wide oblong of glass.

'Not know why missee not sleep,' Lotus said. 'All velly proper to sleep now. You been wakey all night.'

Christina shook her head miserably, but felt comforted that Lotus stayed near. Lotus was only a fraction smaller than herself, her face lovely and unlined for all her twenty-eight years. When Christina's mother had died, it had been she who had mothered and adored the missionaries' tiny, pretty child.

'Would care to listen to unworthy self?' Lotus asked. 'May speak?'

Christian wearily shook her head, forgetting in her distress that shaking heads in China meant Yes and that nodding meant No.

'Honourable father Morrow, he say he name Mission House after muchee consideration, muchee care and very long and proper thought.'

'It hardly matters now,' Christina said sadly. 'I don't think anything matters very much now.'

'Matters! Honourable father, he say we must watch and see how tall and strong the mountain lilies grow. He say they not mind even wild breezes, they have such fine strong stems. They grow and multiply no matter what hardships they find and no matter how poor the earth. Golden lilies grow pure and strong, no matter what the odds, he say, like faith!'

'And like his love,' Christina whispered unsteadily. 'But now it's over and done with. Father is dead, and I feel that a part of me has died too.'

'He gone to Other Country with honourable ancestors. He happy with old friends and with the beloved

Ann. He no longer weak and in pain from insides. Is good!'

'I—I'm glad his suffering is over.' Christina felt the ache of her loss grow into a dull pain in her heart. Her lips trembled as she added, 'And—and I hope he is in the heaven in which he so devoutly believed. A lovely, shining, beautiful heaven, Lotus.'

'Is wonderful and happy place, better than here,' Lotus said stoutly. 'Where all is noble and is always plenty rice. Is best to believe in *all* celestial places, though. In that way, cannot go wrong.'

'Oh!' Christina smiled faintly at that. 'How incorrigible you are! And father truly believed that he had converted you.'

'He not really believe that. He say, Lotus wayward childs—like missee.'

'How—how understanding he was, and how kind. Oh, Lotus, it's not possible that he is gone.' Great sad eyes were like dew-drenched violets in grief as Christina held her opened hands palm upwards in anguish. 'It's simply not possible!'

'Sleep now,' Lotus insisted gently. 'Is proper. Is best.'

'I cannot sleep, and—and I cannot take this emptiness, Lotus. In a way I will be relieved to leave—to leave this place.'

'Beloved and honourable missee must not leave!' Lotus's eyes gleamed with frightened distress. 'Not happy in any other place.'

'It—it is not up to me, dearest; you know that. Anyway, staying will be too painful for me now.'

'You come back?'

'Perhaps. One day.'

'Honourable father, he say work must go on.'

For perhaps the hundredth time, Christina tried to explain. 'I am not, nor have I ever been, a missionary, Lotus. Neither am I a nurse. I am not on the books of the Foundation, and all in good time they will send someone else to carry on here. I will be told to leave. That is how it is. Those are the facts!'

'Beloved and honourable missee went back to own country to learn new things at school,' Lotus said obstinately. 'She cried many tears. Sent many letters to honourable father. She say she not leave ever again. That Flowery Kingdom is real home.'

'I was allowed to return because of father.'

'Your other land too far away, muchee too far. Here you are in centre of world. China is heart of the world. You makee good lady nurse. You help many childs. You help far too many childs!'

Christina smiled sombrely. Everything Lotus had said was true, and it was making the situation that much harder to bear. Also, she had indeed taken in four new children after her father had died. Who would look after them now? Poor Lotus really could not grasp the truth of the situation.

James Morrow had indeed begun the Christian Mission House of the Golden Lilies, but the work would have been impossible without the help and finance of the Christian Mission Foundation. She, Christina Morrow, was of no concern to them at all. She had come here of her own free will, to be at her father's side. She helped him as best she could, and in her spare time she read and studied all the books and pamphlets written by the famous and indestructible Florence Nightingale, the great and marvellous British philanthropist and hospital reformer. Christina felt she knew all the rules of the 'Lady of the Lamp' off by heart. Because of this, she herself had been able to help in a good and practical way. She had! In all probability she could do more than any new person sent to run Golden Lilies—a lot more! But officialdom would never accept that.

Christina found it in her heart to hope that the Foundation would not send someone like Miss Emily Worthington to replace her father. She tried to suppress her sense of guilt at the thought, but was unrepentant.

Miss Worthington had a closed mind and was as narrow in outlook as many of her ilk. She was a hard-faced no-nonsense lady based in Peking, who was absolutely certain that her way, and only her way, was right. Her own unquenchable faith was the only one to have. She believed quite sincerely that it was her bounden duty to convert the teeming millions of China. No matter if they be prince, peasant or pauper, it was all the same. Every single one of them needed to be saved from their nasty dirty ways!

By this time, 1899, white foreigners in China were legion, and many seemed quite determined to look down their noses at the 'ignorant Chinese'. They over-looked the fact that China was already a land of culture and grace when the English amounted to a few blue-painted tribesmen. Even the opium smoking was hardly the ordinary Chinaman's fault. It suited the Miss Worthingtons of the world to forget that the East India Company had been fiercely determined to flood China with poppy-dope purely for commercial gain; to dismiss the fact that the old Chinese Emperor had fought tooth and nail to stop the import of opium during the 1840s but had lost that battle. The Company had been as greedy for profit, Christina thought, as the missionaries were now greedy for souls. One way or another, it really did seem that China was being gobbled up!

Father had been in a class of his own, Christina thought wistfully. He had neither prated nor preached, and he believed quite simply that actions spoke louder than words. So he had fed the poor and healed the sick, and he had given out large helpings of hope where there had been none before. He did not try to steal souls, only to gather them gladly when given, and had been as equally prepared to let them go. Now he himself was gone. Even though his passing had not been unexpected, Christina was numb with grief and shock. She felt immensely alone.

She wanted to hate China, to loathe and detest it for

its strange back-to-front, topsy-turvy ways. But she could not, for she deeply loved and cared for her adopted land.

Unable to sleep as Lotus wished, she decided to go out and visit one of her father's oldest and dearest friends. Madam Way lived in a lovely house just inside Peking. Lotus tried to protest, but Christina had her way. Clearly distressed, Lotus went off to order a palanquin.

CHAPTER TWO

CHRISTINA WALKED THROUGH the mission gate and pulled her coat about her. For all it was spring and the bitter winter gone, her thickly wadded cotton coat was necessary. So were its wide sleeves, inside which she tucked her hands to keep them warm. Under her coat she wore a serviceable heavy-weight brown and beige tweed skirt, a high-necked beige blouse and a brown woollen cardigan. She had put on long leather boots. For all the thickness of her clothes, Christina still looked frail and strained, with purple shadows under her violet-blue eyes.

Golden Lilies was situated a mere half-*li* outside Peking's outer wall. It was the only major capital in the world not located on a river, but during the sixth century it had been connected by canal to the sea and to the fertile grain province of the south. But Christina was barely noticing or thinking about these things. She was finding the world too incredibly sad.

They came to the great gate, that was not so much an opening as a fortress—rather like the huge 'pylons' the ancient Egyptians had built. Soldiers guarded the entrance and also lived in the fortress above. If one were left on the wrong side of the gate after nightfall, when it was closed, it would take an army to get back in. But it was still early, and many people were heading towards the city. Farmers bearing their produce in baskets at each end of shoulder-poles, merchants heading caravans of camels, women and children hurrying and scurrying to and fro with enormous baskets filled with good things balanced on the tops of their heads. It was 'bright morning', 'good joss time'. The runners carrying Christina jogged with their quick loping strides along the curved bridge over the canal, and on to the gate. There, they were waved on through the gate, and all about them swirled the mass of life and noise and bustling activity that Christina knew so well.

Many white people mingled with the crowds: Americans, French, Japanese, British and others, all standing out, with their different clothes and mannerisms, from the pigtailed and conical-hatted Chinese. The bearers jogged down narrow streets where the buildings were so close that their slanting roofs all but met above. People, busy with the business of the day, happily jostled past shops with gaily painted red and gold signs hanging outside the doors. Pawnshops, numerous and crowned with distinctive towers, were as busy as ever. Vendors cried aloud the perfection of their wares.

At last the bearers came to a quieter part of the city and stopped before a green-painted door. Christina alighted and went over to rattle the bunch of hanging brass petals to announce her arrival. There was no latch outside, or handle. Typical of China, the door must be opened from within!

She smiled as she heard the wooden crossbar being lifted, and someone pulled apart the two heavy doors. A young woman servant whom she had never seen before helped her to step over the high threshold board, and then led her past the low kitchen set to the left, whose large oven filled most of the floor space, then over the sill of a Moon Gate, a pretty circular opening of bricks, finally to the path to the right. Here the woman stopped.

'Madam Way, her pavilion,' she said, quite unnecessarily, since Christina had visited this charming place many times before.

'Thank you,' she replied, and smiled at the young woman, who kowtowed in a sour, mutinous way and returned to her own domain.

Christina walked towards the long, single-storey building at the far side of the court. Its heavy roof sloped downwards to the centre, and it was situated, Chinese fashion, on a terrace raised a yard up from the flagstones which paved the court. In this manner, ground-damp was overcome.

A short flight of steps up the middle of the little terrace led to a glass door, now standing hospitably open. As yet, surprisingly, Madam Way had not appeared. The front of the pavilion was very pleasant to look at. The supporting pillars were painted red, as were the beams under the roof. There was a continuous series of oblong window-panes set in a wooden lattice. Where there was no glass, there was a soft cream-coloured Chinese paper with a fine silky water design. Pots of newly awakening shrubs made an avenue for Christina's feet as she passed up the terrace to the door.

Suddenly her steps faltered. Her heart was fluttering in her bosom like a frantic bird. There was something wrong! Why had Madam Way not yet appeared? There was now something horribly hypnotic about that silently waiting, open door. She wanted to go through it, yet the hair at the nape of her neck was prickling. She pretended an interest in a rather beautiful plant-holder that she had admired many times before, glancing swiftly round from under lowered lids. To all intents and purposes she was alone; even the gate-woman had disappeared. So why did she have this incredibly eerie feeling that she was being watched? I am being too silly, she told herself firmly. Madam Way must be busy, or visiting relations. She was not expecting me, after all. If she were at home, she would have come out by now, to welcome me . . . But why the open door? She must be here.

It did not make sense. Madam Way recognised every sound coming from the outside world and every tiny song the hanging crystal windbells made. They tinkled merrily whenever visitors came. But the most loved sound of all, for Madam Way, was that of the courtyard gate opening, for it meant visitors. When that happened, she clapped her hands and called to Tsu. And Tsu, of rough, peasant stock, would smile and bob, and help his

mistress to walk the few paces necessary to the door.
Madam Way could barely hobble unaided because of
her tiny crippled lily-feet.

Christina took one more step. Then, behind her, the
gates were splintered open with a crash, and a man's
English voice ordered sharply,

'Stay where you are!'

She froze, and had a confused impression of a small
group of Legation guards running after a large Englishman straight into the house. Her hands flew to her
mouth to hold back her scream. It seemed that all hell
had broken loose—either that, or she was going out of
her mind! There came a high-pitched babbling, and the
sound of a shot. Then five coolies were hustled outside.
They were mouthing and screaming obscenities, their
eyes so wicked with hate that Christina's blood ran cold.
And, over all, her mind was screaming the question,
'What has happened to Madam Way?' Without pausing
to think, she ran into the house. Then she stopped short,
and her hand flew to her mouth to stifle her own awful,
heartbroken cry. Madam Way had been murdered, as
had her old retainer Tsu.

Horrified beyond belief, Christina could not tear her
eyes away from the fragile, beloved face that was so still
in death: away from the china-fine hand whose fingers
were still looped round a pearl-handled fan. Dear God,
she could not look away from the long, slim, waxen
fingers still holding the fan . . .

'Pull yourself together!' a crisp voice snapped. 'I said,
take hold of yourself. You had no right to come in here.
Are you quite mad?'

She heard the voice, but still could not look away from
that poor dead little lady. Then, as sick realisation came,
she opened her mouth to scream, but it was nipped in the
bud. Strong, vice-like hands were on her shoulders, and
she was being shaken long and hard. She gasped,
fighting for breath now, utterly helpless in the relentless
grasp. Then she was all but marched out of the house

into the courtyard, until she was standing, gasping for air, under an old mulberry tree.

Tears came. Terrible pain-wracking salt droplets that turned the world into a blurry haze. Try as she might, she could feel the hysteria rising within her and began to cry out, but could only gasp again as her senses were shaken back with ruthless brutality. With an effort, she gained her self-control and stood there, gulping air, fighting to find a composure that she was sure she would never feel again.

'Good!' the man said at last. 'Save your tears until you can blub all you want in the privacy of your own home. It will do no good to lose face and show weakness here.'

Ashen-faced, she stared up at the cold-eyed stranger. He was in his thirties and had wide shoulders and slim hips. His voice was that of a man used to authority. His face had rugged good looks, and under the wide-brimmed slouch hat she saw that his hair was dark. His eyes were brown and piercing. He wore an open-necked civilian shirt beneath his riding-jacket, beige breeches and high tan boots. His lips twisted in a tight furious smile as he went on, 'You know the situation out here. You had no right to travel alone. You should be ashamed of yourself! I have better things to do with my time than worry about the likes of you. You are to get back to that mission of yours, here and now. Do I make myself clear?'

As a strong arm went round her shoulders, she flinched, but she was marched willy-nilly through the courtyard and out of the gate. The palanquin-bearers were called forward. Their faces were expressionless.

'The Mission House, chop chop!' the man ordered. 'And I had better not get there before you. If I do, there'll be trouble!'

They said nothing, but merely stood there while Christina was bundled into the curtained box. At the man's order, they lifted her up in unison and began to make off in quick, jogging strides. He had stepped back, dismissing her without a word. Christina was vaguely conscious of his rudeness, but in no frame of mind to care. All she wanted was to get back to Lotus and give way to her fresh heartbreak and sudden inrush of terrible fear. She was still dazed when the bearers set her safely down before the mission gate. As she walked through into the courtyard, children came running forwards to greet her. People bobbed their heads, smiling, then got on with the business of the day. They were warm, friendly Chinese people, and she knew and loved them all, but now she had to get away. Had to hide. Had at least to pretend not to lose face.

Ignoring even Lotus, Christina went to the sanctuary of her room and threw herself down on the bed. She lay staring up at the ceiling for a very long time, shedding no tears, and all her emotions seemed to have drained away. There was merely a dazed sense of nothingness, and everything around her—even the likeness of her beloved father on the shelf under the mirror—seemed unreal. As did the washstand on which stood a water-jug of white china decorated with pink roses, and a basin edged with gold. The black japanned cupboard that held her clothes was decorated with pink butterflies, as was the serviceable chest of drawers. It was a small room where nothing matched, but once it had been warm and homely with its desk and shelves crammed with books. Now it was like a suspended world, cold and remote and nothing to do with her at all.

But reality returned at Lotus's incessant scratching at the door. She got up, and walking with a kind of rigid care, went outside to join her dearest friend. Lotus took one look at her face, raised her brows, and said, 'Talky-talk good for the soul. You tell Lotus what wrong. Will help.'

Wordlessly, Christina followed her into the main room, where tea had been made. Lotus shooed a group of children away, and they went out, laughing, their eyes dancing, but Lotus's were full of concern as she set about pouring tea in the small and delicate cups.

At last Christina found her voice. 'Lotus,' she whispered through ashen lips, 'I still cannot believe that —that I saw what I saw. It was horrible . . . Horrible! I—I went into that house because I heard—heard this awful shouting and screaming, and—and because of the . . . I—I saw dear little Madam Way, Lotus. She —she was dead! Killed! Tsu was there too. He must have fought like ten tigers, but they had finished him off. They—they looked like broken statues, Lotus, and —and all I can think of is Madam Way's hand. She—she was still holding her fan. The one with the mother-of-pearl handle that I—I gave her, and . . .'

Lotus firmly placed the cup of tea in Christina's shaking graps. 'Missee drink,' she said. 'Drink while hot.'

Christina sipped at the tea, her wide, pained gaze still fixed on Lotus, even though she was seeing Madam Way in her mind.

'Lotus, I do not understand!' she gasped. 'Why did they murder a dear, sweet little old lady like that? She harmed no one, no one at all. She was concerned only with her flowers and her paintings and the song of her birds. Oh dear!'

'She was Rice Christian,' Lotus said flatly. 'Allee same, I Rice Christian. They hate!'

'Are we really and truly deserving of such malevolence?' Christina lifted her stricken face to look pleadingly into the wise almond-shaped eyes. 'Oh, darling, what is the world coming to? I am almost afraid to face the future. I wonder what the future will bring, in fact. I—I wonder if I'm going a little mad, or sleep-walking, and will wake up to find that everything's all right.'

'May speak?'

'Since when . . .' Christina smiled in a faint, watery way at that. 'Since when have you not spoken your mind?'

'Much wisdom come from Confucius. He say, *Study*

past if you would divine the future.'

'Oh, but I don't understand.'

'Many mens angry. Angry as before. Did many wicked things and made two wars. They make Opium War. They make Taiping War. Now war allee same.'

'Oh!' Christina said again, and suddenly felt too weary and sick at heart to want to speak more.

'Not know too much about these things. Lotus cares only about little missee. She take tea now. Rest.'

Obediently, Christina sipped at the pale China tea. While she did so, she tried not to dwell on the horror of the day, but the only way to drown the horrendous picture of the present was to remember the past. And every waking moment of that had been concerned with loving and helping her father, learning from him, admiring him for his selflessness and his open adoration for every living soul in the world.

It was getting late, and the distant walls of Peking were a faint dusky smudge against the sky. A vast stretch of darkness was hiding the flatness of the great plain. The purple void on high had a million tiny holes cut in it through which shone the light of the stars.

'I like to imagine your mother singing and floating among the stars,' James Morrow had said. 'It all looks so beautifully clean and honest up there—and Ann had such wonderful silvery eyes.'

And Christina, who could barely remember her mother, had nodded in agreement and wished momentarily that she, too, had silvery eyes rather than the deeper violet so like those gleaming in her father's sensitive face. But nothing she could ever be or do would ever lessen his pain at losing Ann.

'Please, oh please,' Christina whispered. 'Let them be together now, walking peacefully hand in hand.'

In a vague way she heard the high chirrupy voice of the gatekeeper. A moment or two later, the whispering of Lotus's cotton-slippered feet. Then, with a sense of shock, the clear clipped tones of the man whose whip-like warning had stopped her from taking the last few steps into that silently waiting house of danger. He had saved her life, but he had also shaken her and shown her the utmost contempt. Suddenly she felt too disheartened and depressed to worry very much about that. She heard his brisk footsteps, then saw his outline against the door. She could sense his snapping dark eyes piercing the gloom before he ordered, 'We'll have some light in here. This place is as black as Hades.'

How dared he! A faint shaft of anger split the greyness of her grief. She stood up, very slowly and gracefully, then walked across the room to stand before him and look into the darkly etched lines of his face.

'Please go away,' she said quietly. 'Even though I owe you my life, your coming here is an intrusion, and your attitude is unforgivably rude.'

'For ordering some light on the subject? Come now, Miss Morrow, don't act so unreasonably. As for saving your life, no thanks are necessary. You were merely a rather silly lady hovering there—and quite in the way! Oh, and for what it's worth, I'm not the sort to chose to live in a dungeon. I cannot abide gloom.'

'This is private property, Mr . . .'

'Doctor. Dr Alan Kingsleigh. And as for this being private property, I understand that this in fact is God's house? Shouldn't it have open doors for all?'

'This is not a church, Dr Kingsleigh.' She was trying desperately to keep her temper now. 'Golden Lilies is . . .'

'For heathens alone? Come now, Miss Morrow, we are all sinners in our different outlooks. Oh, and off the record, I have very little time for missionaries and their prying, interfering ways. In many respects I believe they're causing incalculable harm.'

He turned and clapped his hands, calling loudly for lights. He waited, and with obvious satisfaction watched as the boy Wu set down two large, brightly gleaming oil lamps. Then he turned back to Christina, and for the first time saw her tired and careworn face. His expression softened.

'Oh dear!' He put his arm round her shoulders and led her firmly towards a chair and made her sit down. 'I am indeed unforgivably rude, and I need a swift kick for my pains! Forgive me for being so brusque. For all my detestation of the situation here, I should not have forgotten the courtesies. My name is Alan Kingsleigh. I am only recently attached to the Legation's chief medical officer who, in turn, despatched me to this place.'

He was bristling with anger, and she was fervently hoping that he was not the man who had been sent to replace her father.

'Put you through it rather, haven't I?' he asked. 'I apologise, Miss Morrow. I didn't expect to find myself up to my neck in mayhem. I was sent along by the Legation johnnies in case there was any medical need for me. Then, when I realised the situation had got out of hand, I took over. I was rattled, and I admit it. We'd been warned about the proposed attack on Miss Way.' He cleared his throat irritably. 'To be frank, it wasn't my idea to go rescuing a Chinese lady whose sin, so I understand, was to spread the Christian word. But what did throw me was to see you, a young Englishwoman, standing there in the direct line of fire.'

'You are a doctor?' she asked evenly, finding that she was capable of grasping only one fact at a time. 'Your duties must be far removed from those of my father, yet he was a doctor too.'

'Far removed?' Near-black brows were raised in a quizzical way.

'My father's concern was for the Chinese, their poor and sick. Not the rather self-opinionated ladies and gentlemen in and around the Legation.'

He frankly grinned, and there were twin devils dancing in his eyes.

'Bravo!' he said, 'A very spirited reply. One that

shows exactly where your loyalties lie. But, to be very honest, even some of the most high and mighty are pretty nice people when one gets to know them.'

'I never said . . .'

'They have nothing to prove, you see,' he went on, obviously neither hearing nor caring about what she had intended to say. 'It's the jumped-ups, the all out get-to-the-top-quick people who go out of the way to tell the world how superior they are. People who are out of their class.'

'Class hardly matters at all out here, Dr Kingsleigh.'

'Well, it does in the Legation. Even doctors' wives are very aware of their position in the scheme of things.'

She shrugged wearily. 'I am not very kindly disposed towards your "pretty nice people", Dr Kingsleigh. My father spent his days and nights looking after things as best he could here. When his limited funds ran out, he would sometimes send distress signals to the better-off. He very seldom received any replies for his pains.'

'Distress signals?'

'Begging letters,' she replied starkly. 'It was quite amazing how many fine ladies were either out or else indisposed when it boiled down to handing over a small sum.'

He was staring at her intently, then drew up a chair and sat down opposite her. Having studied her drawn face and defiantly lifted chin in silence for a moment or two, he said evenly, 'My dear Miss Morrow, how very, very angry at life you are!'

'No,' she replied tightly. 'Not at life. People! When no one helped—and father's "best" did not seem good enough, when the very last farthing had gone . . . Well —well, he tried harder, that's all. And he hung on to his own brand of faith. I—I used to want to weep, watching him try to bring about the impossible. My father was a devoted, gentle person who would have died for his faith, yet he devoted his time to that of feeding and healing bodies rather than fishing for souls.'

'He was a quite remarkable man,' said Dr Kingsleigh. 'I had heard of him almost from the moment I arrived. He was thought of very highly by those who matter. As for his begging letters, I believe that a certain Dr Strangeways did in fact help as often and as generously as he could. This, when his own pockets were usually emptied on behalf of abandoned Chinese children.'

His tone held a rebuke, and she flushed because she felt he believed her to be saying that her father was the only saint-like person around. Had she been implying that? she wondered wildly. Was she already putting father on a pedestal a million miles high? Ranking him alongside angels rather than remembering him as he was, a quiet, charming, dedicated man?

'Dr Strangeways has all of my admiration and respect,' she said, almost too quickly. 'He used to come here whenever his duties allowed. He and father enjoyed an occasional game of chess.' Her voice quickened, became a little too high as she continued, 'My father achieved great and wonderful work in which sheer faith played a major part.'

'I am quite sure,' he replied.

She knew that she was boring him, and that she was repeating herself, but once she had started, she couldn't stop. For the life of her she could not stop! She went on, her voice hurried, breathless. It was as though she were running a race that had no finishing line.

'I have watched my father throughout the years. I have seen him graduating from total reliance on quinine, Epsom salts and laudanum to an informed use of native herbs and remedies—and achieve miracles! There is a herb, ginseng. Have you heard of it? It has been used here for well over 5,000 years, and father . . .'

'Stop it!' he said sharply.

'A number of mythical tales have been built up around it, and it's shaped like . . .'

'I said, stop it. Stop it now!'

'My father—you don't understand, he . . .'

'Now!'

She gasped, then stared at him, confused, suddenly aware that she had needed him to put a stop to her rising hysteria. She found that she was unsure of herself, of the world and just about everything in it.

There came a scratching at the door, and at her breathless invitation it slid back and a group of grave-eyed children came in, all looking very neat, with well scrubbed hands and faces. They ranged in age from two years to twelve. Some of the boys' heads were shaven, as custom demanded. Others wore the traditional pillbox hat. They had on blue padded tunics and cotton trousers. The girls' trouser legs were worn loose; the boys' were neatly bound by white cotton strips from the calf down. The girls were especially enchanting, like little dolls with their thick black fringes, or else hair pulled tightly back from their foreheads and plaited in one long thick pigtail. With one accord they went to Christina and stood as close as they could, their backs to her, for they were staring wide-eyed at the forbidding-looking stranger.

Using all the will-power in her command, Christina took in a deep breath and pulled herself together. She had to, for their sake!

'You may go to the box,' she told the children, her voice holding all of the loving care in the world. 'Honourable Lotus has told me that every single one of you has been most deserving today.' The puckish-looking twelve-year-old Wu, clearly the leader, was smiling and bobbing now. He headed the file of children as they walked across the room. On the low table was a large red-laquered box, its sides decorated with four snarling gilt dragons. Wu, with careful ceremony, opened the box, which contained prettily shaped wafer-thin maize and honey cakes. With much sticking out of tongues and intense concentration, each child finally chose one, beamed at Christina, kowtowed first to the stranger, then to herself, and left the room.

'They're the same the world over,' Alan Kingsleigh said wryly. 'Needing just a little care, and the occasional treat.'

'I—I know. It is not very much to ask, is it?'

His eyes went over her in a purely professional way. 'You should not be here,' he said abruptly. 'You should be sitting in one of the fine Legation rooms taking tea and eating ridiculously small iced cakes. You are much too young and inexperienced to cope with the situation that is developing out here.'

'I was born here, Dr Kingsleigh. I am perfectly at home in this land.'

'My dear girl, I know all about that!' His tone was exasperated. 'But you saw what happened to Madam Way. Don't tell me that you're as deaf, dumb and blind as the authorities round here! They'll have to wake up some time. They don't even admit that the Boxers exist! Do you?'

She bit her lip at that. Oh yes, she believed they existed! She had seen a group of them, and they had brought fear to her heart. Instead of the mushroom-shaped hats most men wore, they had tied red cotton squares around their heads, and there had not been a pigtail in sight. About eight of them had arrived, and it had been their intention to put the fear of God into her father. They had jogged into the mission compound, and their movements were unnatural. They took great strides, sometimes forwards and sometimes moving from side to side, giving the impression that they were almost dancing. Their fists were clenched as they made strange boxing movements with their arms. In spite of the cold, they had not worn the usual padded jackets but red open-necked shirts, and their feet were bare. But it was not the way they had dressed that had been so awful, or the crab-like menacing walk-dance, it had been their eyes. Staring, fanatical, self-hypnotised. Her father had stood before them, quiet and calm. If he recognised the leader as the husband of a woman whose life he had saved only a week before, he did not give it away.

'Foreign devils,' the man screeched. 'Foreign devils go home!'

'I am a man, just as you are a man,' her father had replied. 'I am your brother under the skin.'

'Filthy pig! Excreta of goats. We will take off your skin. We will cut out your heart, and while it is still beating, we will burn you alive.'

'And while I am burning, I will be praying to my God,' James Morrow had replied. 'And the peace in my soul at that time will outdo any agony that you or your men can inflict on my bones. Now go and do your prating elsewhere. I don't want you around the place when Officer Wainwright arrives with his men. He is due almost any minute now.'

Officer Wainwright was well known in the area. Red-faced, pig-eyed, he was ill-tempered and cruel to his men. He was infinitely worse to the luckless Chinese who crossed his path. He and his equally detestable wife loathed China, and the lowly people who had to serve either of these hard barbarians feared and hated them. Mrs Wainwright had died from a fall some months before. The Chinese servant, whose duty it had been to escort her safely through the streets, had chosen that time to disappear. Officer Wainwright swore that it was murder, that all Chinks were devil's spawn. Faced by men such as those gesticulating and mouthing at James Morrow now, he would, without any compunction, order them to be mowed down.

Even as James Morrow spoke, there had come the sound of a troop of horses advancing. The Boxers, mouthing and hating with their eyes, had melted away . . .

'You believe they're just another harmless secret society, don't you?' Dr Kingsleigh snapped. 'Ye gods, are you as blind as everyone else round here? Is it possible that you don't understand that the Empress herself is behind all that they are doing now? That she'll back them in all they intend to do? And I was given to understand that you had your finger on China's pulse. That you were not as stupid as most!'

The colour sped to Christina's cheeks. He was glaring at her. Well, if he expected her to cringe, he was going to be disappointed! She sat up very straight and cool. 'If you're insinuating that we are surrounded by enemies, Doctor, I must confess that I'm rather more afraid of those called Hunger, Ignorance and Disease.'

'Bravo!' he exclaimed as he leaned back in his chair and folded his arms. 'An actress could not have handled her lines better. But, Miss Morrow, the time is coming for a rude awakening. And when you consider how outnumbered we are, it is not brave to dismiss the idea of danger. It's stupid.'

She smiled coldly, then said with an air of dismissal, 'It really is late, Dr Kingsleigh. I must ask you to leave.'

'I am sorry, ma'am,' he replied, and settled himself more firmly. 'And it is not all that late.'

Her colour deepened, her large eyes grew frosty. 'I must insist, Doctor,' she said even more firmly. 'Please forgive me for not being able to . . .'

'Entertain me?' She saw the twin glints of devilment gleaming at the back of his eyes again. 'That will not be necessary. Please accept that we shall have to learn to live with each other. I am not about to leave here at all.'

'I'm afraid I don't understand you!' Her anger was growing, and she was wondering whether to call for Lotus and get her to bring the men to get this—this person out of the way. 'Until my father's replacement arrives, I have every intention of continuing his work here. I am quite capable of managing mission affairs on my own. Now, if you will excuse me, I . . .'

Quite ignoring the fact that she had jumped furiously to her feet, he said, 'The sad reality is that Paul Aubrey was held up by rioters just outside Feng-tai. Your Mr Li was with him the last time they were seen. They were riding horses rather than using the railways, and, I'm sorry to say, have been neither seen nor heard of since. It has been decided by the Powers that Be that I must stay here and help all I can. I am, in short, here to take Paul Aubrey's place.' He smiled briefly. 'I understand that he's a very likeable young chap. You'll no doubt have him twisted round your little finger from the word go, but I'm a different kettle of fish. I am a doctor, and a dedicated one. As to the Chinese soul, I believe each man to his own.'

It was an open reproof. She saw it as such, but the enormity of what had gone before outweighed everything else.

'You can't stay here, Dr Kingsleigh. Surely you are needed in Peking?'

'It has been agreed, by those in a position to have their own way, that a young English girl cannot stay here alone.' He raised his brows in a quizzical way, 'Of course, there is an alternative. You can pack your bags and come back to Peking with me.'

She shook her head furiously. 'No! I intend to stay here and wait until my father's replacement arrives. But I do not see that you . . .'

'Since that's the case,' he cut in, 'I must tell you that I am the only man that can be spared. As a newcomer, I am virtually a free agent. So, like or lump it, I'm here, and here I'll stay!'

'You're being too kind, but it's all unnecessary and —and . . .' She glared at him defiantly, 'And you don't have to humour me, so please don't use that rather false parental tone. I don't believe that we need a kind of guard here. What is more . . .' She was going to tell him that there were quite a few men in the near vicinity who could be called on should the need arise, but he cut in on her again.

'My dear young lady!' Her head flew up at that. The man was insolent, almost too insolent to be true. How dared he! He went on quite unabashed. 'Please stop being an ostrich and accept that we're heading for a decidedly sticky situation. The death of Madam Way should have convinced you of that. She lived inside Peking—not out here alone.'

He's a beast, she thought, an unmannerly beast who seems determined to cut off ruthlessly everything I am trying to say—and why must he keep on about Madam Way? He hasn't a feeling bone in his body, and I don't want him here!

'You won't be able to practise properly, don't you understand?' she flared at him. 'Our standards here are merely basic, and you'll find the work uninspiring, our space quite inadequate, and . . .'

'I mean to start out on the right foot with you,' he told her, not even trying to hide his impatience. 'I have arrived here very unwillingly from a place called Kishna Komari, in a part of India's jungle. It has a corrugated iron roof that holds the heat and smell, just as this one must in its equivalent Chinese way. Only here it's spring, and so dust and sandstorms are the order of the day. Over there it's heat and wet, mildew, snakes and scorpions and a million other disgusting things. In fact, I'd say that Kishna Komari is way out on its own.'

'Then how is it that you come to be here?'

He was suddenly extremely angry. His eyes snapped and his voice became hard, almost cruel. 'I was outclassed and out-manoeuvred every inch of the way. But that's no concern of yours. Please have your boy show me to my room. I believe my luggage has already been brought inside.' He glared back at her, snapping, 'I have no intention of sleeping on the floor! I shall, of course, take over your father's place.'

'No!'

'It is not unnatural to want a room of my own,' he told her. 'Since I understand there's nowhere else, your father's quarters it shall be. Please call your boy and have him understand that I am in the position of authority here. We might as well start as we mean to go on.'

Seething helplessly, she rang the little bell that sig-
nalled Wu. He came, bobbing and beaming, ready and
anxious to please and adore. Wu would be falling at Dr
Kingsleigh's feet in no time at all, she was sure. He had
been devastated at the passing of James Morrow, but
death was quite acceptable, since it led to a happier way.
Now there was a newcomer to placate, and the puckish
little boy was a past master at getting his own way. He
would kowtow and grin from ear to ear and dog Alan
Kingsleigh's footsteps and become as indispensable as
only he knew how. And why not? Christina's good
honest self asked. If life can get a little easier for the Wus
of this world, why not indeed?

She found it in her heart to hope that Alan Kingsleigh
would be kind to the boy. There was a great deal to like
about young Wu, especially his painstaking care of the
small children he had taken under his wing. Like them,
he had been abandoned as a baby and left to die.
Christina found herself trying desperately to concentrate on Wu, on the tiny ones, on mission chores waiting
to be accomplished on the following day. But it was no
use. Everything now seemed incredibly wearisome and
sad.

She watched as Wu led the awful Alan Kingsleigh out
of the room and to her own beloved father's place. It was
sacrilege, she thought, and drew in a deep shuddering
breath. She sat disconsolately in the chair, wrapped her
arms round herself and rocked backwards and forwards
in a silent paroxysm of grief. There was no father, no
Madam Way, no official position in Golden Lilies for
herself. Even Lotus belonged, and would be employed
here for the rest of her life; father had seen to that a long
time ago. He had not 'tied' herself down in any way at
all. He had, he had said, wanted her to find a man to love
and be as happy with as he had been with his own dear
wife. But there was no man. In every way, she was in
China on false pretences. She had no permit to work
with the mission. She was now, just as she always had

been, merely her father's child. Now father had gone, she was on her own. Dr Kingsleigh's attitude had quite underlined that fact.

A sliver of hope came then. So, the new missionary, Paul Aubrey, was a good sort! Kingsleigh would not have said that had it not been true. He was only held up—he would be arriving some time, perhaps soon! She was not unattractive, she knew the work . . . Suddenly Christina perked up. She had a mission in life—to get a man! One who would marry her, and allow her to continue where her father had left off. She felt a thrill of excitement and daring as she tried to picture the man she planned to marry. What did he look like? How far away was he? What was he doing now? She was glad that Li had gone to meet him. They would be back that much sooner. Paul Aubrey, she whispered the name. She tried to imagine the face of her husband-to-be.

That night, before closing her eyes, she whispered plaintively, 'Where are you, Paul Aubrey? Why don't you hurry? I have such plans for you and me.'

Sea Jade left the filthy little room where Paul Aubrey lay and went outside to the courtyard. Near the wall was a mud shrine, which held a small clay figure wrapped in a little red cotton shawl, the presiding spirit of the water supply. On either side of the shrine, red paper strips were written over with ideographs. These asked that the blessings of heaven and earth might rest on the water. In the little mud pot which stood before the figure was a pinch of incense-ash left from the offerings of travellers.

Since the Inn of Great Security and Content was set outside and quite apart from the village, the innkeeper seemed to have few local friends. His standard of life was extraordinarily low, and he seemed to be living in a kind of mental torpor most of the time. His wife was as quiet and as slow as he, and she had the coughing sickness. They were both openly cowed by authority and were openly afraid at even the mention of Han Shen's name.

Sea Jade had disliked and distrusted the innkeeper on sight. She felt sorry for his wife. Mostly, though, survival was on her mind.

To all intents and purposes she was alone in the harsh world. She must care for the white man, whom she found so very attractive, because of his helplessness. In spite of herself, and because of him, she must also care for the pathetically loyal dog. It had been a crazy thing to do, sneaking out of the inn to look for Rayn, she knew that now. Anything could have happened, and she had weakened her own position by acting as she had. But the look in Rayn's eyes had been enough. She was glad she had gone out to rescue him. Fiercely, wonderfully glad!

She shivered, remembering her interview with the innkeeper first thing that morning. She had walked into the long, dark, filthy communal eating-room, with a hardened earth and stone bench stretching from one end to the other. The innkeeper had been squatting on it, his face blank. He took no notice of her.

'You will make food for honourable guest, please?' she had said.

'Filthy barbarian not honourable,' he had replied in a flat voice and turned his soulless black gaze on to her face. 'Putrid dog not welcome here.'

She had felt ill at that. So he knew that she had sneaked out last night to get Rayn! Someone must have seen her, although she had honestly believed the gods had been on her side. She had been sick with relief when she had reached the gate and found the old gatekeeper still snoring, the wooden door still a little ajar. How careful she had been, creeping inside, getting Rayn to wait while she replaced the long wooden bar. Tiptoeing, almost, to get the dog inside, almost weeping when she had seen how weakly but lovingly the beast had crawled next to his master and then closed his eyes.

'Putrid dog is here,' she said, and her voice was cool and sure for all the frightened uncertainty that was churning in her. 'Barbarian is here. Own humble and

lowly self here—all on honourable business for a personage high above. Therefore it is auspicious that we
eat.'

'Eat dog.'

'Dogmeat not fit for barbarian. Make him sick. Big
dog is friend of devil-man. Be wise to remember that.'

He was narrowing his eyes, not liking a mere woman
daring to argue with him. She knew that the situation
was getting very bad, then inspiration came. 'If not
treated all very proper, will send for the great lord Han
Shen.'

'Do you want it watery or stodgy?' the innkeeper said
swiftly, his eyes shifty in his face.

'Stodgy,' she replied, and wondered just what her
next step could be. The barbarian was still helpless and
in fever, stretched out on the filthy mattress with Rayn at
his side, the great dog now looking as if he also would
soon expire. On seeing them in the first light of dawn,
something in Sea Jade had reached out to them both.
She was now trying to help them, not because of the
direct orders from Peking, but because she wanted to.
The first thing, though, was to get them back to health.
The Inn of Great Security and Content did not live up to
its name, but it was better than nothing and, for a while
at least, she was safe.

The innkeeper, who had left his wife in the dark
stuffiness of his bed-living room, stared at Sea Jade, then
with a shuffling movement got to his feet and went to the
end of the room where he plied the tools of his trade. As
he did so, his wife put in an appearance. She neither
looked nor spoke to her husband and totally ignored Sea
Jade. She made her slow, wheezing way to the hovel
where the carters of the night before had slept. It was
still littered with the rubbish they had left. The woman
fetched water, and sprinkled the mud floor and the bed.
Then, picking up her besom, made of stiff desert grass
tied round a stick, she began sweeping. In spite of the
water sprinkle, clouds of dust made the air like dry

yellow soup. She began to cough in a harsh and rasping way.

The innkeeper turned up the ragged cuffs of his old wadded coat, took a bowl and began morosely kneading flour and water, then quickly and skilfully, he used his long, slender rolling-pin to spread the lump of dough into a large thin sheet. This he folded into many layers, which were finally chopped into strips and tossed into boiling salted water.

Sea Jade, now sitting on her heels and resting her elbows on the eating-bench, watched him carefully. She did not trust the man, though what he could do to harm her and the white man was hard to tell. When the food was cooked, he ladled it into three bowls made from plaited, varnished bamboo, and placed them on the bench. He set a pair of wooden chopsticks by two of the helpings and placed a wooden bowl of coarse salt near by. He then walked back to his own room, and his wife followed. Sea Jade was left to manage the rest on her own. Since there was no tray, she carried the dog's food as well as Paul's to their room, then returned to get her own—just in time to see the innkeeper scooping at the bottom of the cooking-pan for the pastry strips he had deliberately left there. It seemed that he and his wife would eat at no expense to themselves for the day. So that was all! Relieved and smiling a little, Sea Jade went back to the room.

It took a long time to get Paul to eat one or two pastry strips. She had to break them into tiny pieces and all but push them down his throat. His eyes were glazed, and he seemed totally unaware of what was going on. Rayn's nose twitched at the smell of the food. He opened his eyes, and his ears began to lift. He ate wolfishly. When man and dog could eat no more, Sea Jade began her own sparse meal. By the time she had finished, Paul had gone into an uneasy sleep, his hand resting on the dog's head. Rayn had gone back to his old position close to his master's side.

Knowing that they were both best left in peace, she wandered into the courtyard. The inn, though warm enough, was stifling, and it smelled. She needed to breathe in some fresh air. As she moved towards the door, the inkeeper appeared, blinking and glowering.

'Lodging, attendance and water money, missee,' he demanded.

'All paid when we leave,' she replied. 'And I will give extra for the care of the dog. We stay. We stay perhaps one more time.'

'Pay now!'

'When we leave.'

'Leave now!' He was looking ugly, and she knew that he wanted her out of his place. It was dangerous for him to shelter such a strange trio, and he was getting to be mortally afraid.

'We stay one more time,' she said, then added for good measure, 'Lord Han Shen, he sent us here. Lord Han Shen would not like to hear that you sent us away.'

The innkeeper gave up, but she could feel his eyes watching her even now. She continued to stand before the water shrine and wondered, for perhaps the thousandth time, just what she could do. Her orders had been to keep the Aubrey Paul away from the mission until she had become indispensable, but what was the situation now? The missionary's injury had been inflicted out of a personal hate that had nothing to do with Peking's great plan. Such was the man's wound that he was beyond reasoning. Much of the time, he was hardly aware that she was present. He was in no position to choose his companions or make his way to the mission house by either the longer or the shorter route. In fact, there was nothing he could do about the situation. It was all up to her!

A cry came from outside the wall, and the innkeeper appeared and watched while the old gatekeeper shot back the long wooden bar. The mounted newcomer was one of the look-out men who had vanished on the night of the attack. So, she had not been abandoned, after all!

The newcomer and the innkeeper began to haggle at the tops of their voices about the price of a meal, but reached agreement at last. The wife with the coughing sickness shuffled off with the horse. It was she who set about chopping sorghum leaves for the animals and who gave the horse a bundle of dried desert grass and led it to the old mud-brick trough.

The man, short and long-faced, his hair shaven back from his forehead, his pigtail worn long and loose, walked to the shrine. He lit a joss-stick before the water spirit, then said without looking at her, 'Honourable Miss Ling Sea Jade, she is to return to father's house.'

'Oh?' Sea Jade was startled. 'I am not to go to Mission of Golden Lilies?'

'All finish. Man who knew all necessary things, he finish. He die. Miss Ling Sea Jade not necessary to plans now.'

'And—and the barbarian?' Sea Jade asked, her mouth suddenly going dry with fear. 'What is to happen to him?'

The man turned to look at her then, his face expressionless. 'He no longer missee's business. He stay. He make way best he can.'

There was no further argument about it. Sea Jade was left where she was, standing before the water spirit, while the man strode to get his meal. So, her mission was over. All she had to do now was to pay the inkeeper and leave. The barbarian and his great black and yellow dog were no longer her affair. They could make their own way to the Golden Lilies Mission—if they were not murdered first!

She shivered, and her small hands trembled pathetically as she brushed her hair away from her face. What to do? She could not leave the missionary, she knew that. Nor could she leave the dog. She would at least stay at the inn for one more night, and in the meantime she might get some idea of how she could get them all home.

To the House of Ling? No! That could bring terrible trouble to the people she loved because there was one certainty in all this. The barbarian and herself were no longer small cogs in the wheel of the Empress Dowager's plans. They were expendable. So Sea Jade was in this on her own, and the Aubrey Paul? He was a hated Christian missionary and, left alone, he would be cut about and killed as horrendously as had his old friend Li—this in spite of everything the courageous Rayn could do. There must be a way to stop that. There must!

Trembling, Sea Jade crept back to the man and his dog. As she entered the room, Rayn looked up at her with his big, true eyes.

CHAPTER THREE

SEA JADE TOOK a bowl of water to the dog, and while Rayn drank, she rested her hand on his long thin head, her finger scratching behind his ear. 'I will not leave you,' she told him quietly. 'I will do all that I can for you and Aubrey Paul, but I must pray. I must beg of *Yesu* and August Personage of Jade to help us. The master is no better. Is not good!'

She leaned anxiously over Paul, her heart sinking. It did not take an expert to see that the injury he had received was serious. Apart from the dried blood in his ear, the wound on the side of his head was deep. His skull had taken a terrible blow, and—in spite of his brief moments of consciousness—Sea Jade recognised that he was, in truth, more dead than alive. Her puzzlement grew. She had responsibility now, but she was as helpless as before.

Her mind went back to that other life: the safe, gently sweet, life in her father's house. She had spent most of her time in the women's courtyard, the Well of Happiness, with the other fine ladies of the house. High-born, they were waited on by a staff of servants. They whiled away their leisure hours with much gossip, music, laughter and pretty fluttering of fans. They enjoyed parlour games, and fashion was a great delight and concern. They loved music and painting, also dancing. They fussed over and loved their little pet birds. Sea Jade was always made much of, and she was called upon to play the flute that was, so far as she was concerned, inseparable from life. It was all a million miles away from the existence of the peasants; she could see that now, whereas she had never thought much about it before. She squatted next to the mattress, her hand now looped in Rayn's collar, her mind busy with thoughts.

A peasant and his family lived in a draughty one-room house with a tiled roof, a dirt floor and no furniture. Half his meagre crops went to the landlord who owned the fields, and another large part went to the government. To feed his family he had to trap small animals, and catch fish and frogs if there was water near. Peasants, out of poverty, were often forced to sell their young children as servants or slaves. Sometimes it was necessary to kill their babies because there was not enough food—and always and ever, no matter how badly they fared, the tax-man came with his clenched iron fist. Taxes had given rise to the proverbial saying: 'An oppressive government is more terrible than tigers.'

The Empress cared nothing for this. She had spared no expense to rebuild the Summer Palace that had been sacked by the British in reprisal for Chinese aggression during the Opium War in 1861. The whole area had been rebuilt, and palaces and other beautiful buildings abounded. Canals and little ornamental waterfalls and pools were everywhere. The Empress's demands had been insatiable. With money that had been set aside to build a navy for the nation, she had had a marble pleasure-boat erected in her grounds. It was magnificent, and was paid for with five million ounces of silver extracted from her impoverished subjects for the construction of warships.

In spite of all the secrecy, hints of the Empress's extravagance were leaking from the court. A new faction grew, of people wishing to see the end of her reign. There were some who hated her almost as much as they hated the foreigners who were taking over the Celestials' land. With such a sad state of affairs, Sea Jade thought, who could be trusted? There were those who would be ready and willing to kill her for her audience with 'T'zu-Hsi alone. Perhaps Ling Fu would suffer as an accessory to the plot the Empress had dreamed up. And for those not concerned with thrones and dynasties, there was universal detestation of the white mission-aries. She was between the devil and the deep blue sea, and probably no one in the world would be willing to help her. No one at all.

Unbidden, the vision of Lord Han Shen came into her mind. He had helped her before. Would he help her again? But it was unthinkable that she would be allowed to approach such a man. Not even as the honourable Miss Ling Sea Jade could she go uninvited to his house, let alone in her guise of a peasant girl. There must be a way—there must! Han Shen, the noble, the august, the most handsome of men, was her only hope. Sea Jade found herself whispering into Rayn's quivering ear.

'Have money. Must find coolie willing to take mess-age. Must pray to the gods that coolie not take our copper coins and run away.'

The tip of a tail wagged, and Rayn lifted his head and yawned before resting his head on his master's chest again. But his eyes were on Sea Jade, and once again she found herself drawn to the animal that had so terrified her before . . . And the white barbarian? Confused, she realised that he affected her in a very strange way.

Han Shen was a man of strong personality, impressive appearance and exemplary good taste. He was skilled in the arts of horsemanship, archery and polo playing, and learned in the noble skills of calligraphy, astronomy and music. Unlike most of his kind, he took a keen interest in the people on his estate, and was therefore looked up to as a god. The peasants were afraid of him and his power, but, unlike his dead father, Han Shen was a humane man. He kept a stern eye on the provincial magistrate who toiled at the essential tasks of collecting tribute and taxes. He did his best to help the very poor, and had, during exceptionally bad times, supplied them with grain.

Now he sat alone in his garden. It was quiet and peaceful, this mild evening. A small breeze teased the windbells, and their whispering melody was sweet in the air. Han Shen relaxed with his pipe, a look of thoughtfulness on his face.

Only that morning, fresh instructions had come: the plan had been changed. There was no need to concern himself with the odd couple he had had taken to safety to the inn on his own vast estate. The reason for their protection no longer existed; it was dismissed. The two were no longer of any account.

Slightly relieved, he had gone about the business of the day, but to his annoyance, he had been unable to put the peasant girl out of his mind. She was beautiful, with an air about her that intrigued him. He had taken only one swift look into her large expressive eyes before she had fallen to the ground in the customary kowtow, but it had been enough to shake him out of his usual complacency. The women in his life were the accepted chattels he had inherited on his father's death, some of whom, being rather younger than himself, he had enjoyed. He liked women, but had found himself unmoved by any special one. He had never fallen in love. Poets extolled the virtues of true love, the gods smiled on lovers. It was a very necessary emotion, it seemed, but not to him. He was happy as things were. He was young and strong, and as yet felt no particular desire to sire sons. All was right and correct with his world. He drew long and slow puffs at his pipe, and tried to give himself up to the peace and beauty of the garden. But it was not to be. His mind was alive with memories. Treacherous ones, perhaps, but they were there; they always had been there at the back of his mind.

Han Shen thought of the old Dragon Woman who so determinedly and so bloodily held on to the throne. She had spent all her adult life grasping at power and holding it tightly in her bony, long-finger-nailed hands. She could and did outwit all who dared to stand in her way. Princes, mandarins and generals who had tried to oppose her were killed, their heads sliced off their shoulders with ruthless efficiency. Some, who were popular with the people, were done away with more discreetly. Thus had a distant cousin of his own perished. Distant so far as blood was concerned, but close as a brother in affection and respect. The young man's death had been a painful one. Bad fish, it was said, but most knew that it had been poison. Han Fei had openly said too many things about the Dowager Empress and her spendthrift ways.

'China's economy is more important than ornamental lakes!' he had cried. 'The Empress has embezzled the funds of the nation. No wonder China's navy was defeated by the monkey-men of Japan! The Empress has squandered enough money to build a dozen navies. Is the woman on the Dragon Throne absolutely mad?'

This and many other disparaging things had been said by the fiercely nationalistic young Han Fei, and so he had had to die. Han Shen's eyes went bleak at the memory, and the corners of his fine strong mouth turned down.

There came the sound of high-pitched pleading at the gate, and the caustic reply of the gatekeeper determined to send someone away. But Han Shen heard the words 'peasant girl' and 'barbarian', and sent a servant to find out what the commotion was at his door. A few minutes later the man came running and threw himself down in supplication before his lord.

'What is it?' Han Shen asked coldly.

'A coolie, lord, a low and despicable person not fit even to come near the shadow of the wall of this house. He is a wretched creature who should have expired before attempting . . .'

'What does he want?'

'Oh, lord!' The servant was wringing his hands and kowtowing in distress, since his master's displeasure would fall on his own thin shoulders rather than on the upstart gutter-wretch whining outside. 'This—this creature bears a message which he dares to say is for your ears alone.'

'Then bring him to me.'

'But, lord, he is a lowly and incredibly unnecessary creature. How can such as he have a message worthy of your ears? How can you bear to have such a devil's rag-picker in your own honourable presence?'

'I can bear it,' Han Shen said with a faint, wry humour. 'Even if you cannot. Have the man sent to me, and then leave us. If I need your help, I will call.'

In fear and trembling the servant backed away, bobbing and weaving, his face miserable, his eyes distressed. His livelihood and that of his whole family depended on his master's good mood. The coming of a coolie to the house was a very unusual occurrence. Such a fetid creature could only be the bearer of bad joss!

Moments later a ragged wretch, emaciated and with eyes set deep in his painfully thin face, was all but kicked to a sprawling position before Han Shen. He lay, shivering and abject, quite beyond speech of any kind.

'What is it that you have to tell me?' Han Shen asked sternly.

'Oh, lord, it is good of you even to glance at my lowly and humble self. I would not have dared even to approach the door had the young girl not been so insistent. She gave me money, lord, and said that I shall have more when I get back. The money will feed my mother, my wife and my children, lord, and will get a new coat for my honourable great-grandfather who is all but dead with the cold. Oh, lord, the money will . . .'

'I do not wish to hear all this. Give me the message.'

'It is from a young peasant woman, lord, and she—she is with a filthy barbarian goat.' The wretch's voice rose high with terror, for he expected a blow at any moment for having allowed such awfulness to escape his mouth. 'I beg the lord to forgive me for even mentioning such obnoxiousness, but . . .'

'I shall have your tongue cut out if you don't give me

the message at once!' Han Shen said, and looked as if he meant it. 'What did the peasant girl say?'

'She—she asks for your help, lord. She said, "Please help".'

'And she gave no indication of how I could help her?'

'She did not say, lord. She most explicit. Say to the Lord Han Shen, "Please help".'

'I see.' A faint smile gleamed momentarily in Han Shen's eyes. He found himself not displeased at the thought that the girl had turned to him. She had audacity and courage, that was clear—and also immense foolishness. He could be anyone, anyone at all. He could have her killed merely for speaking his name. As for the barbarian . . . His mind went back to his beautiful image of the girl. A peasant—but a jewel for all that!

'Go back to the person who sent you,' he told the snivelling coolie. 'Say that the Lord Han Shen will consider the message.' He clapped his hands, and the servant came forward and without ceremony began kicking and pushing the man away.

'Let the man carry away a small sack of grain,' said Han Shen. 'See to it that it is good, nutritious grain, not the stuff that you give the birds and the beasts. This man has many mouths to feed, and grain is food.'

The coolie fell to his knees and began screeching his blessings, but Han Shen's eyes were staring over the man's head, unseeing. The interview was at an end. Old Wang came then, muttering at such misplaced generosity. Han Shen smiled, for the old man had been a close and trusted friend of the family since long before he himself had been born, and his great-nephew Wang Ch'ung was his own dear friend.

'It would have been misplaced generosity to give him money, Wang. That would have gone in opium or gambling-dens. He will not sell the grain. He will not dare! It holds the mark of Han on the bag, and there are many who would tell us if the grain was not properly used—in hope of a reward.'

'Your generosity to such a low . . .'

'That is enough, Wang! Leave me to my thoughts.'
The old man all but melted away.

Han Shen folded his arms, hiding his hands in his
sleeves, and began to consider what was best to do. The
girl and the barbarian were nothing more than an embarrassment to him now. If he was sensible, he would have
them thrown off his land, yet he hesitated. The barbarian was of little or no account, but the girl . . . She
was another matter entirely! He was curious about her.
Her manner was not actually that of a peasant. She had a
veneer of refinement that hinted that she was used to
living, not in a mud hovel, but in an educated person's
house. A peasant would never have dared to take that
one quick look up into his face. A peasant girl would not
have such an air of delicacy and refinement. And a
peasant girl's hands . . . That was it! It had been there
all the time. No wonder he had been unable to get her
out of his mind!

The young girl had, quite clearly, never done a day's
work in the field in her life, neither had she lifted heavy
weights and walked for miles with them balanced on her
head. So! The old Dragon Woman had been particular
about choosing her pawn—her obsolete pawn now, it
would seem. The girl was a lady, no less!

It came to Han Shen that it might be of some small
amusement to talk to her, to find out a little more about
her. But she must not know what was in his mind. That
would never do! She must not be on her guard at all.
Perhaps she was rather more devious than she had
appeared. After all, she had been at the Iris Pool on the
Empress's orders. His long fingers tapped thoughtfully
against the stem of his pipe. Perhaps it would be wise if
everyone believed that his interest lay solely with the
Englishman. Yes, that would be best. He clapped his
hands, and waited. Old Wang came running.

'At first light,' Han Shen said, 'you will see to it that a
litter is sent to the Inn of Great Security and Content for

the white man who is staying there. He is to be brought here.' He added, almost too casually, 'Also, if she so chooses, the peasant girl attending the barbarian may take shelter under my roof. She, too, may ride. It is not necessary for her to walk.' He paused significantly, then added, 'Even though the journey would not be too difficult on those unbound feet of hers.'

'Lord,' Wang began in alarm, 'it is not good joss to welcome a white devil here. What is more . . .'

'If you want your head to stay on your shoulders,' his master cut in silkily, 'you will waste no more of my precious time.' Old Wang vanished.

Han Shen sat where he was, smoking his pipe and contemplating the willow trees, the rhododendrons and the little toy bridge that arched its way delicately over the ornamental stream. A movement in the shadows of a screen of bamboo made him look over his shoulder, but it was merely the fluttering of a bird coming to roost. However, it reminded him that there were enemies everywhere.

He knew that the Empress would soon learn about the barbarian he was about to take in; and, of course, the girl. He had received express orders to forget them both, to allow them to make their own way. It was his duty to kowtow to the Dragon woman's wishes, to carry out her every instruction in an unthinking, instantly obedient way. So far as T'zu Hsi was concerned, it was not auspicious to have subjects with thoughts or wills of their own. Step out of line, and the punishment was likely to be swift and sure. With great deliberation, Han Shen clapped his hands. A servant almost as old and as trusted as Wang approached and kowtowed.

'Tomorrow we are to have a visitor,' he said firmly. 'Prepare the best place for him. There will also be a girl.' He remembered those pale hands that had never tilled or hoed, and a faint twinkle came to his eyes. 'She is to be fed, and tasks found for her—those that are deemed suitable.'

*   *   *

It was strange, Sea Jade thought early the next morning, how swiftly things had begun to happen. The coolie had returned quite late on the previous evening, all but overcome with the great and adventurous thing he had accomplished.

'The Lord Han Shen, he say, "Will consider message",' he had quivered. 'He very fine man!'

'Thank you,' Sea Jade had replied, and felt despair. It would have been more honest if the 'very fine man' had replied with an outright No.

For the rest of the night she had crouched near to Paul, and listened to his fevered mutterings that made little or no sense. She tended him, and found comfort from the growing devotion of Rayn. The dog had accepted her now, and she him. With nothing but instinct to guide either of them, they had become friends.

Morning came, moist and misty and pierced with gold. Sea Jade, after a last despairing look at Paul, went in search of the innkeeper. She found him at his place near the bench, by the meagre cooking-fire. There was water boiling. Around the man were set the basins, platters, tea-blocks, minute screws of salt in blue paper, small pinches of tobacco, wooden ladles and chopsticks, and a very few but very necessary supplies.

'Tea?' Sea Jade enquired politely. 'Is possible?'

His eyes were spiteful. 'No tea.'

She held up a coin.

'No tea,' he said again.

She held up two coins, then firmly, 'Tea!'

Unwillingly, he put a scraping of tea in one of the crude earthenware teapots and swamped it with hot water. He placed this and two basins on a tray, then, with a slow insolence, deliberately turned his back.

Shocked at the insult, Sea Jade said quietly, 'Your ancestors must be writhing in shame! They must be like shrivelled dried leaves blown away before the wind of your disgrace.'

He swung round at that, his face distorted with hate.

'No!' he said in a low guttural voice. '*Your* shame—Rice Christian!'

She gathered up the tray with shaking hands and hurried back to where Paul lay, looking as if he had not moved. He remained so still that she gave a pain-filled little cry as she sank to her knees beside the mattress. She placed the tray on the floor and poured the tea. Then she very carefully slipped her hand under his head and raised it so that she could hold the tea-basin to his lips.

'Come,' she pleaded, 'must try! Must drink. Is important that you get well.'

'I—I'm so sorry,' he mumbled, but his eyes were barely focusing, and he tried to turn his head away.

'Is good!' she insisted. 'Is hot. Must try!'

It took a little while for her even to begin to get through to him. And she was suddenly aware that her heart was acting in a quite peculiar way. He reminds me of a picture I saw once, she was thinking, of a Christian holy man. A saint who had hair of gold and just such a lean and noble face—a Western face with the same broad forehead, the same strong nose. Eventually she managed to get him to take a half-basin of the tea, then he groaned and gave up.

As she slipped her arm away from supporting him, he muttered, 'Give—give the ol' boy a drink. He—he's a decent . . .' He fell back helplessly, only semi-conscious, on the filthy straw again. It was Rayn who had the lion's share of the tea!

The closeness, the smell, the sheer lack of any semblance of fresh air made Sea Jade seek escape once Paul seemed to be asleep. Wearily she walked to the courtyard again. It was as wretched as ever, a most depressing place. She began pacing up and down, stopping every so often before the water spirit. But there was no inspiration, not even there.

Suddenly there came the sound of rapid hoofs. They neared, then stopped outside the compound walls. A loud voice called, 'Open up! I am Wang Ch'ung, head man of the Lord Han Shen. Open up, I say!'

The old gatekeeper hurried, and was almost knocked down for his pains. Banner-men came, waving the light and dark blue of the House of Han, then guards, led by a flat-faced, thickset, very distinctive-looking man. Sea Jade shrank back and felt as afraid as the innkeeper looked as he came scurrying.

'Show us the room set aside for the special visitor,' Wang Ch'ung called out. 'We are here to take the barbarian with us.' He paused, then added in threatening tones, 'It is to be hoped that the white man has been treated well under this vile and disgusting roof!'

In spite of his attitude, Sea Jade thought that perhaps Wang Ch'ung's bark was worse than his bite. Even so, she did not have the courage to step forward, but pressed her back hard against the wall. The innkeeper was kowtowing as rapidly as a clockwork toy now, and screeching that the gods had blessed him by sending such grand and glorious visitors to his humble abode.

'Get on with it!' Wang Ch'ung said impatiently, and motioned to the panting bearers who had just reached the gates. As instructed, they went inside the inn, while Wang Ch'ung and his men waited. A few moments later Sea Jade caught a glimpse of the litter-bearers going at their loping run through the gate. One of them had torn trousers, and there was blood on his leg.

Wang Ch'ung watched them, his eyes narrowed. He was a squat, firm figure who looked well on his tough mountain horse. He gave an order to one of his men, who hurried to the innkeeper and told him something that delighted him, for he began kowtowing again and crying aloud his thanks to all the gods and the noble personages of the House of Han. Wang Ch'ung was not listening. He grinned and said something vulgar to his men, who guffawed in a rough and jolly way.

'Not so!' The innkeeper's joy was short-lived. 'Was promised money for services. How can I survive if I am not paid?'

Wang Ch'ung's mouth twisted in contempt as he threw down a small heap of coins that constituted a small fortune in the innkeeper's eyes. While the man threw himself down to scrabble frantically in the dust, he said in an icy voice, 'My master should know the truth. This place is a pest-hole, and people should be paid to keep away from it! To my mind, this inn needs to be burned to the ground. Breathe one word about the barbarian, and I swear that I will put a flame to it and also to your own disgusting self. Do I make myself clear?'

'Lord, may my soul be ripped out. May my ancestors rot in . . .'

'Ah so!' Wang Ch'ung cut in, and spurred his horse round so that he now faced the trembling Sea Jade. His eyes twinkled, and his lips curled up.

'Come, girl, you are to ride with me.'

She could not move and, was suddenly consumed with panic. She now realised that she could not be sure that Han Shen was a friend . . . he could be the very reverse. Her plans could perhaps already have gone horribly wrong. She had been foolish to believe that the great and powerful nobleman would help. Indeed, he might have ordered the death of the white man already! He might be making even worse plans for her own humble self. She had not only dared to stand in a foreign devil's shadow, but tried to help him as well!

'I am not going to bite your head off, girl,' Wang Ch'ung said good-humouredly.

With a single, strong movement he swung her high and placed her comfortably behind him, then gave an order and they all began moving through the gate on to the track leading directly to the north. Just before they began to pick up speed, the innkeeper's voice could be heard shrieking and shouting.

'Stop! Stop! It will not stay. My blow did not finish it, and for all it belongs to me, it will not stay.'

Sea Jade looked back, and cried out at what she saw. The innkeeper was literally jumping up and down, waving a wicked-looking cleaver over his head. Ahead of him, Rayn, with tongue hanging out and staggering, was endeavouring to follow them.

'You said it was mine!' the innkeeper screamed. 'It tried to kill me! Help me to slaughter it. In the name of the gods, I ask . . .'

Sea Jade threw herself off the back of the horse and found herself somersaulting painfully on the ground. Unaware of anything but the need for haste, she picked herself up and began running as fast as her legs could carry her, desperate to get to Rayn in time. She reached him and fell to her knees at his panting side, her arm going round him in a protection.

'So sorry,' she whispered. 'Not think! Good ol' boy.'

Wang Ch'ung came riding up, and he was not amused. 'Do not waste my time, girl! Leave that disgusting creature and come with me.'

'Forgive, please,' she whispered, remembering in time that it would be safest and best to keep up her humble peasant façade. 'This is Rayn. He have name, and he dear to barbarian's heart.'

'I had no orders about a dog. Leave him!'

'So sorry,' Sea Jade stammered, pale-faced and shivering, for she knew that it was quite within Wang Ch'ung's power to cut her down. 'I gave word to Christian that I would care for his dog.'

'You dare to argue?' The man was clearly amazed. 'You, a lowly woman who is honoured even to be mentioned or thought about by honourable and noble Han Shen?'

She remained miserably silent, still holding Rayn.

'There is to be a meal waiting for you and a place set aside in the servants' quarters. You do not deserve such consideration, yet you defy me! Will you lose all hope of a future for the sake of a disgusting creature that has seen better days?'

'Forgive, please,' she faltered, and kowtowed low so that her forehead touched the dust. 'Is very wicked of me. I crave forgiveness for impossible behaviour. Must stay with dog. Gave promise. To break word would be to lose face.'

Wang Ch'ung snorted impatiently, and made as if to lean over to swoop her once more on to his horse. But she jumped to her feet and stepped out of his reach, while Rayn growled deep in his throat. They stood looking up at him, girl and dog, vulnerable yet pitifully defiant. Wang Ch'ung's expression softened a little.

Seeing this, Sea Jade pleaded, 'If honourable gentle-man forgive audacity of own humble self, might not Sea Jade and dog make own way to house of Lord Han Shen?'

'You would get lost. You are a female alone in the hills with men who have not enjoyed a woman for a very long time. The dog is large enough to feed an army of rebels, so he would have his throat slit in no time. I cannot allow you to attempt such a journey by yourself.'

Sea Jade knew that she was fighting a losing battle. The man could not be blamed; he had received orders from the master, and those orders must be carried out. Why had the noble Han Shen not made provisions for Rayn? Perhaps, she thought, he also looked on the dog as a source of meat for the hungry. Poor Rayn—how different it would have been had he been ugly and tiny with a fluffy tail and squashed-in face like the little pet animals favoured in Peking—so favoured that they were bred nowhere else and bore the name of Pekinese.

The innkeeper's greed was getting the better of him. Rayn would indeed feed a great number of people, and for such a luxury as meat, the carters would pay a good price. Thinking of this, he dared to stake his claim again—at the top of his voice.

'Animal is mine! Animal payment to keep still tongue in head!' He had managed to say exactly the wrong thing.

Wang Ch'ung fixed him with a contemptuous stare.

'Get back to your pest-hole, you disgustingly greedy toad! If the girl speaks the truth, that she gave her word to care for the beast, there is nothing more to be said. If she has lied, my master will cut out her tongue and you may have the pleasure of eating it. Now, get out of my way!'

Not daring to argue, the innkeeper retraced his steps, nodding his head in utter disbelief at his abandonment by the gods. Wang Ch'ung now turned his attention to Sea Jade.

'The Lord Han Shen was most insistent that the white Christian be taken to his house. You were merely an afterthought. A place has been prepared for you out of the kindness of his heart. There was nothing said about this yellow devil, and I have the feeling that it will bring about your end one way or another. But I must warn you that, if you do not present yourself, with or without the dog, at the house of my lord and master, things will not go well with you. You therefore have a choice.' She looked up at him, pleading in her eyes. 'You will choose either to ride with me and hope that the creature can keep up, or you will make the journey on foot.'

'Oh, thank you! I will walk gladly,' she replied, and was unaware of how lovely she looked, tired and dusty though she was.

'My master will no doubt order that you and that creature be killed for complicating what was to have been a simple matter.'

'I—I will walk in honour,' Sea Jade stammered. 'And with every step I take I will pray for the Lord Han Shen's understanding. And I will pray to the gods for you.'

'For me, girl?'

'That you have good joss for all of your days, O great Wang Ch'ung. I will never allow my lowly self to forget how kind and good you have been to me.'

'Be careful,' he growled. 'I might decide to join the men in the hills who have not eaten the fruit of a woman.

You look ripe for the picking, girl! Perhaps I shall call on you when you are safely closeted within the walls of the house of Han.'

He wheeled his horse round and rejoined the waiting men, singling out one, who left the group and waited for Sea Jade. He was tall and thin and young, with set and angry expression. To be picked out to stand guard over a peasant and stinking animal was not auspicious. He would lose face when the tale got out. He sat on his horse, rigid and unfriendly, waiting while Sea Jade slipped her hand through Rayn's collar and began whispering to him to walk. The journey to Han Shen's home began at a very slow pace.

As they went on, Sea Jade began to wonder about Paul's condition; whether he was still alive and perhaps missing her. What had made the noble Han Shen relent? How was he treating the white man, who was now so helpless and in his power? What was her own future to be?

A picture of Han Shen leapt unbidden into her mind, and her heart raced with an excited kind of fear. How handsome he was, distinguished and proud. How attractive! The women of his house, and she was sure there must be many, were fortunate indeed. It must be a delight and honour to be allowed into his bed, and a blessing from the gods to bear his son. He was truly an honourable man. One that would not stoop so low as to hurt a helpless missionary, she reasoned, and felt comforted by the thought.

Thinking of the puzzlement and pain in the white man's eyes made her blink back the tears. How was it, she wondered, that a person she had not known existed could move her so deeply? She remembered Paul's pain-filled, dazed blue eyes, and the tender gentleness of his hands as they had cupped her face in a gesture of gratitude and trust. She would never betray that trust. Never! Somehow she must get him safely to the Mission of the Golden Lilies and to his own kind. Then and then only then could she return with honour to the dearly beloved House of Ling.

This led Sea Jade to wonder about the vagaries of Fate. She was a living epitome of conflict. She was devoutly Chinese, but her early years had made her sympathetic to many Christian outlooks and ways. She loved and revered the aged, gentle Ling Fu, but also she loved and adored the memory of the Fairweathers. Both blue-eyed, incredibly patient and kind, no one could have wanted for better parents, and her heart still ached over the loss of them. They had brought her up to be courteous and ladylike, to have an enquiring and knowledgeable mind. They had taught her, and the Lord Ling Fu had continued her education in the knowledge that that was what his English friends would have wished. It was the blue eyes, so like those of Mary Fairweather, that had drawn her to Paul Aubrey—or to the Aubrey Paul, for to be good Chinese was to use the surname first. Now she was again playing two roles in life. She was member of a high and noble household, but living the part of a lowly girl belonging to no home at all.

If she safely reached the place of Han Shen, she must forget her love of fine and beautiful things. Must not give away her knowledge of painting and poetry and her understanding of writing. Must not play her flute—for peasant girls had no time for such a useless occupation, the rule being that of never-ending toil. Sea Jade bit her lip at the realisation that her 'place', if there was to be one in the Han household, would be lowly indeed. Her tasks would be menial. She hoped devoutly that the Number One Lady of the House was kind. If she was not, daily whippings could be the order of the day. Suddenly, very fiercely, Sea Jade wanted to kick up her heels and run. Run anywhere, do anything, except take the long walk to the establishment of the Lord Han Shen. But to be a coward was not good Chinese. And she was Chinese in heart and soul and every fibre of her being.

Sea Jade's fingers tightened round Rayn's collar, and she was glad of the feel of the furry body walking so close at her side. She knew she must go through with the charade. She must bide her time, think and plan. She made a silent vow to the gods, both yellow and white, that she would somehow restore the Englishman to where he belonged.

Then she wanted to die, because there was someone riding like the devil towards them. And that someone was the Lord Han Shen!

CHAPTER FOUR

SEA JADE'S FINGERS tightened on Rayn's collar. For a moment her fear was so great that it felt like a million fingernails tapping points of light into her brain. She was going to be mowed down, she knew it. She had disobeyed the Lord Han Shen's orders to ride with the noble Wang Ch'ung, and her punishment would be severe. Her mouth went dry, her stomach tight. When she closed her eyes, the dull sound of pounding hoofs echoed the racing in her own heart. They grew louder, the sound crashing in her ears, then as rapidly receding.

Han Shen had swept by on his black horse, but had not even glanced at them. Weak with relief, Sea Jade stumbled, hardly daring to believe that she was reprieved. That Fate and the gods had stepped in to help her. The great, the most high lord had not even noticed her own lowly and insignificant self. She found herself taking a deep and abiding interest in the path before her. She must not falter. Must not let the stoical, distant guard see how weak with relief she was! The track began to rise, and as they climbed, the sun grew high. She wondered whether she dared to speak, then, at last, decided to try.

'Is—is it much further?' she asked, and marvelled at the steadiness of her voice.

The guard continued to stare ahead, but he answered her just the same. 'No distance at all—on a horse.'

She digested this in silence for a moment or two, then said in a small voice, 'I am sorry to have caused you so much trouble. I did not realise . . .'

'Do not worry,' the guard said loftily, but his eyes seemed a little less hard and impatient.

'I am afraid I am tiring you,' she said plaintively. 'I know how it must be, to go along at a walking pace when a horse as magnificent as yours can surely race like the wind. So sorry!'

'Ah so!'

She felt a little thrill of returning confidence. She had hit on the right subject, and the man's reserve was crumbling.

'She is a fine creature,' he agreed.

'Her name, please? She is beautiful. Must have name!'

'Dancing Snow.'

'Oh!' She let go of Rayn's collar and clapped her hands as delightedly as a child. 'Is lovely! So fitting.' She looked up then, smiling right into the man's profile. 'May lowly self presume to ask own name?'

He looked down into the smiling, golden innocence of her face and relented sufficiently enough to say.

'Szu-ma.'

'Master of the Horse!' she breathed, and her eyes opened wide with admiration. 'How satisfying to have such a fine and distinguished name.'

The guard's chest puffed out. 'I am Number One Son of Great Warrior!' He was very proud and human now, even permitting himself a slight smile. 'My father served the Lord Han Shen's father, and is now in noble retirement.'

'May the gods shower peace and good health upon Great Warrior for all the days of his life,' she said courteously, but she was puzzled. From what the man had said, he was no humble personage set to guard a peasant girl and see her safely to the lord master's house. Master of the Horse, son of Great Warrior, must surely be among the élite. No wonder he had been angry at his humiliating task!

Her lovely face went a paler shade of gold, and she felt shaky. It was all such a great puzzlement, and things had happened too quickly and horribly. She was filled with despair, and wanted her beloved father very much. She wished she was with all the dear ladies that were as pretty and as necessary as the delicate pink blossom fluttering on the almond trees.

As if he sensed her moment of sad loneliness, Szu-ma said, 'You may ride with me. It is a longish walk.' Then, casually, 'Even for someone without lily feet.'

'Thank you.' she whispered. 'You are very kind. I . . .' Rayn chose that moment to nudge her hand with his poor hot, dry nose. 'But—but . . .'

'What is it?'

'The barbarian's dog. He has suffered much bad joss. Last blow from despicable innkeeper too much! He weak now. My lowly presence gives him necessary courage to continue.'

'He is a fine animal.' Szu-ma said unexpectedly. 'And worthy of your attention. The palace dogs are disgusting little creatures, as small and yappy as a discontented first wife. How they are rated so highly, I will never know.'

'The Pekinese are—are royal!' she gasped, not believing her ears. 'You are very brave to speak such blasphemy, Szu-ma.'

'Yes,' he said crisply. 'Even so, I swear by the gods that those small bad-tempered objects are for decorative purposes only. Playthings for women.'

'They are brave and fierce hunters,' Sea Jade replied. 'At least, that is what I have been told.'

'We are told many things,' Szu-ma replied evenly. 'I have been to the palace, and I have seen what I have seen.'

Sea Jade decided that it would be wise to change the subject. 'You have Dancing Snow long time?'

'Since she was born in my father's stables.'

'So you have had the good joss to watch her grow and bloom. My . . .' She stopped herself in mid-air. She was a peasant, and peasant girls did not have fathers who owned stables—wherein even now there languished a very lovely silvery friend. Dear, sweet Trembling Breeze, who was fine-boned and fleet of foot and gentleness itself.

Thinking of Trembling Breeze made Sea Jade almost weep with homesickness. She had been present at the birth, although it had been neither right nor correct for her to be in the stables at all. But she had known that Proud Lady, her father's favourite mount, was about to deliver. In her worry, she had broken all the rules and slipped out of the women's house and into the stables to be with Proud Lady. She had not realised that Ling Fu would be there before her.

He looked up at her, continuing to crouch in the straw by Proud Lady's head. His parchment-fine skin had crinkled up as he smiled, his pleasure at her concern outweighing his anger at her disobedience.

'It will not be long now, child,' he had said in his high gentle voice. 'Come here with me. We will wait together while Keng, Master of Stables, sees to it that all goes well.'

All had been auspicious, and at the proper time the new-born had taken her first breath of life. Sea Jade had cried with emotion at the little creature's first steps. Ling Fu, who seldom caressed her, forgot his dignity long enough to wipe away her tears.

'How shall we name her?' He asked.

'She trembles, Father. As she takes her very first steps, she trembles like a cherry branch dancing in the breeze. She is the colour of the air we breathe. The air that comes like feathers from our mouths and noses on frosty mornings. Oh, Father, she is so beautiful!'

'Then shall she be Trembling Cherry Branch?'

'No! that does not sound like her at all.'

'Is Breath of Misty Morning more agreeable, perhaps?'

'Oh, Honourable One!' She still had tears of emotion slipping like diamonds down her cheeks. 'May she be Trembling Breeze?'

'She is yours to name as you choose.'

Sea Jade's face became transformed with a wide warm smile of incredulous delight. 'Honourable Father?' she had stammered. 'The—the foal is mine?'

'Just as you are mine,' he had replied with all the courteous gallantry in the world. 'And Trembling Breeze shall be her name. Now go back to your rightful place before Number One Lady finds you missing, and has you whipped!'

She had run away happier than she had believed possible. She was also confident because Peach Velvet, gracious Number One Lady, was mature and mellow and never ever unkind. Trembling Breeze, her heart had been singing. Dear, wonderful, darling little Trembling Breeze is mine! I shall love and adore, and care for, her till the day I die. She is my treasure, my delight. We shall become friends and, one day, when she has grown, we shall race like the wind, as one in our delight. She was brought back to the present by Szu-ma.

'What were you going to say?'

'My—my master had a horse whom I loved. It was a long time ago.'

'Your master?'

'I was brought up in a mission house in Tientsin. Port very busy, all concerned with travelling this way, that way, chop chop. Too busy—busy to notice starving lady with little childs in arms. Barbarian lady, she stop, she see! She gave poor woman threepence. Woman gave missionary lady Sea Jade. All very proper business deal. Sea Jade brought up with kindness. Missionary lady all good and correct.'

'Barbarians! I wish them all to suffer in the Eighteen Hells.'

'Not so bad, Szu-ma,' she protested. 'All white peoples not so bad!'

'They should take their long noses out of Flowery Kingdom. We are the heart of the world, and they are like white maggots eating out that heart. They are barbarians: red barbarians who have black hearts, and the devil lives in their eyes.'

Sea Jade smiled up at the angry young man and

pointed out, 'Honourable Han Shen, he say take sick white man to house. Is noble lord going to cut up the barbarian? Make him into little pieces to feed hungry birds?'

'My lord and master knows what he is doing,' Szu-ma said darkly. 'I only hope that he does not get bad joss for his pains.'

'And so do I,' she whispered, and had a fleeting picture of how wonderful the nobleman had looked as he had raced by on his powerful black horse. She became a little more daring and asked softly, 'May speak?'

'You may.'

'I was wondering what is name of the Lord Han Shen's mount?'

'Dark Messenger. He is a thoroughbred that cannot be matched anywhere else in the world. There are many who would give fortunes for him, but my master would as soon part with his own hands and feet.'

'He loves him just as greatly as you do your Dancing Snow?'

'Yes! A man and his horse are like twin souls.' Szu-ma paused, then looked down at the small, weary figure walking so determinedly beside him. He added, almost roughly, 'Dancing Snow is like part of me. I know her, I can read her, feel her. Because this is so, I ask again, are you sure you would not like me to help you up? There is plenty of room here, and Dancing Snow will think nothing of your weight.'

Sea Jade looked up at him with wide startled eyes. Szu-ma was honouring her greatly, and it would be unseemly to refuse his offer of help—and discourteous to a degree. She wanted to accept with all her heart. Her feet ached, as did her legs, her back and seemingly every fibre of her being, but Rayn was moving even more slowly. His tongue was hanging out, and his soft eyes were glazing over. Szu-ma would never understand if she put a lowly creature's comfort above his own kind, deeply appreciated, offer of help. He would not accept that, to her humble self, Rayn had become almost as important as a being in his own right.

In her mind she heard again the Aubrey Paul's ram-
bling fevered voice. He had been speaking of his dog,
begging her in his stiff, English way to look out for his
pet, saying hoarsely, 'He—he's a terribly tough, loyal
old chap. Do what you can for him, there's a good girl.'
Then he had swum away again in a forest of fever,
making little or no sense, and finally not being conscious
at all.

Small nervous hands held Rayn's collar even more
firmly, then inspiration came.

'Forgive, please!' Then, plaintively, 'Feel sick. Feel
faint! Must not dishonour Dancing Snow by being ill on
her back. Feel I might fall. I did not sleep last night. Did
not eat. Do not feel right in self.'

Szu-ma was gravely sympathetic. It was his bounden
duty to look after and care for the girl until they reached
the master's house, or at the very least until a respon-
sible person came and claimed her. Surprisingly, he
found the situation had some charm after all.

'Then it seems to me you must be very tired and
hungry,' he said.

'Yes . . .' sadly. 'Yes, I am.'

'Very well. Although we should not leave the path, I
shall lead you to sweet water. There you may at least
drink and rest a while.'

He turned Dancing Snow's head, and the horse began
picking her way over stones to the left. In a little while
they came to a place where the vegetation was thorny,
and Sea Jade had to choose her path with care. The
tough growth gave way in turn to a softer green, and then
they came to a narrow gully that was dim and cool, and
water made a ribbon of white satin lifting and falling
over cream and yellow stones.

Dancing Snow made her way down with sure-footed
precision. Sea Jade, holding on to Rayn, slipped and
slithered and tried not to mind the spiteful agony of
stony points digging through the thin sandal soles. Then,

thankfully, they were down, on a level with the cool, gaily laughing water.

With a little cry of delight, Sea Jade fell to her knees, cupped her hands together to catch and hold the water, drank deeply, then dampened her burning face. Szu-ma dismounted, keeping a few paces away, but not taking his eyes off his charge for a second. Rayn and Dancing Snow drank their fill.

Han Shen was angry. It had amused him to go for Morning Ride of Bracing Fulfilment. The fact that Dark Messenger's nose was pointing in the direction of the Inn of Great Security and Content had been just one of those things. He had felt pleased when he saw the litter-bearers jogging along at a splendid pace. The blanket-covered barbarian would be properly cared for in no time at all. A few paces behind the bearers, in noble and carefully controlled formation, were his guards. Fine, strong men with steady minds, quick reactions and unerring eyes when it came to pinpointing targets. Han Shen was proud of his men, and above them all, most high in his esteem, was the Number One leader of the guard, Wang Ch'ung, his friend.

Han Shen was puzzled to see that the peasant girl was not before Wang Ch'ung on his mount. Was Mountain Arrow lame? On closer inspection, Han Shen saw that the girl was not on the back of any horse in the group. Not caring to make his consideration, or his interest, known, he had kept up Dark Messenger's pace and raced by the group as though their progress was no concern of his.

Further on, he saw the lonely mounted figure of the young nobleman Szu-ma, and walking doggedly at Dancing Snow's side, the small, fragile, golden girl. She looked very vulnerable and delicate, and Han Shen was quick to see how lovingly her hand was entwined in the collar of the dog. So! The animal was important to her. He had barely noticed the creature out there by the Iris

Pool, but that had been a mistake. Clearly, he saw now, the dog was of much significance. He cursed himself for not realising it. The girl had aroused his curiosity, when he had never before been curious about a woman.

He pictured again the loveliness of Sea Jade's face. How her body was as slender and supple as the new willow stem. Her eyes had been large and lustrous—but hunted. He frowned, suddenly angry that anyone should frighten her, blind to the fact that her fear had been caused by being faced with himself.

It had amused him to keep well out of sight after that, and to watch them from afar. They had been quite unaware of him, and as they progressed, he paced Dark Messenger to match. Then, to his own chagrin and surprise, the small one seemed to have become lively. She was turning towards Szu-ma, speaking with him, her attitude now being one of a gravely interested child. What could the conversation be about? he wondered. He watched the small one turn to look right up into Szu-ma's face, and a little later she had let go of the dog's collar to clap her hands and laugh pleasantly.

At that moment Han Shen found his affection for Szu-ma fading. The young buck was clearly lacking in honourable awareness. He was concentrating on the young girl at his side rather than on his surroundings. How could he be so stupid? There was danger behind every bush and rock these days, yet there was that young devil clearly content to forget everything except the charm of a small creature's smile.

There was worse to come. Szu-ma was turning his horse's head away from the road. He was heading for Bright Water Stream. Was he quite mad? They were out of sight now, and Han Shen furiously spurred Dark Messenger to go like the wind.

Unaware of the consternation she had caused, Sea Jade was kneeling on the bank, gently bathing the fresh wound that the innkeeper had inflicted on the back of

Rayn's neck. Angry tears burned against her eyes. As if he hadn't suffered enough! First at the hands of the wicked man—whom she hated! She hated all Boxers, and she hated all flat-faced monkey-men who called themselves innkeepers! She lovingly laid her face against Rayn's furry wet cheek.

'Poor ol' boy,' she whispered. 'Poor sweet, very nice boy, eh? Never mind, Sea Jade look after you all time now. Just like the Aubrey Paul say.'

Rayn had been patiently accepting her administrations. The sound of her gentle voice was doing more than anything to make him perk up. Then, without warning, his body stiffened, his ears lay back and he bared his teeth to snarl. He was looking over her shoulder, his eyes fierce with hate.

Sea Jade swung round almost as quickly as Szu-ma, and looked up. On top of the slope were three evil-looking men, in everyday Chinese clothes, but one, the obvious leader, wore a red armband. He held a water-skin; but, clearly, water was the last thing on their minds now. They began descending rapidly, letting loose showers of earth and stones. As they came down, they were shouting and screaming in a high fanatical way.

'Here's food for the taking!'

'A woman! Praise to the gods!'

'Kill! Kill!' screamed the third.

Szu-ma had his bow in his hand, and its string was pulled back tight. His first arrow sped like a winged angel of death, straight into the leader's heart. As Szu-ma shot, Rayn had leapt forward. But before he could fight, or Sea Jade could move, while the two remaining men were still a few paces away, the fracas came to an abrupt end. Both fanatics were stopped in their tracks. All Sea Jade was conscious of then was the look of utter surprise on their faces, the disbelief in their eyes as they fell. Then, and then only, did she see the arrows in their backs!

Shocked, shaking, she saw, outlined against the sky, with the light making a nimbus round his head, Han Shen. He looked like a god astride a smoke-breathing black dragon, Dark Messenger was panting so hard. *Hai!* Han Shen *was* a very superior god, a super-being as high above them as the stars; and, worst of all, he was a coldly furious god. The bow in his hand told all there was to know.

With a trembling cry, Sea Jade fell to her knees and kowtowed, as did Szu-ma. Rayn was fiercely shaking one of the dead men's arms, a quilted sleeve gripped firmly between his strong teeth. He seemed unaware of Han Shen, or if he was aware of such an honourable presence, he was quite unconcerned. His deep-throated growling was the only sound in the gully now.

There was a long moment as Han Shen looked silently down upon their disobedient, unworthy selves. Then, with great dignity, he turned Dark Messenger's head and rode disdainfully away.

'By the gods!' Szu-ma swore. 'We are in trouble! We should not have left the path. Hurry, little one. You must hurry. Once we get to the top, you must ride with me on Dancing Snow's back.'

'No,' Sea Jade said sadly. 'I will do anything you ask, except that. Rayn is like a good friend. He will walk at my side, slowly and with much effort.'

'I would agree,' Szu-ma said as he began leading Dancing Snow up the incline, 'if your dog were as near death as you seem to think he is. But he sprang at those snakes with the strength of ten tigers! Make no mistake about that.'

'Look at him now,' Sea Jade whispered sadly. 'Oh, brave Szu-ma! Just look at him now!'

Rayn's strength had gone. He lay stretched out by the corpses, his eyes closed, his tongue lolling, the wound on his head beginning to bleed again.

'I shall not listen to you,' Szu-ma said. 'You will do as you are told.'

'But he warned us of danger!'

'And my master killed two men that I should have!'

'Only because he was there before you. You had plenty of time to see to them both, and I bow to you, for the fine and brave man you are.'

'We must hurry.' He brushed aside her flattery. 'The Lord Han Shen will time our every step from now.'

He turned away from her again as he led Dancing Snow to the top and to the edge of the track. Sea Jade was glad that the young guard had his back to her. It would not do for him to see how ill she felt, how faint! She did not dare to look at the dead men. She felt sick, as, unbidden, the picture of the poor tortured Li had looked when she had found him spread over the rock. From Li, her thoughts went to the barbarian.

'Oh, beloved gods,' Sea Jade prayed softly. 'Smile down upon the Aubrey Paul. He is dear to my heart. He has the sky in his eyes and the sun in his hair. He has the gentleness of good spirits in his touch. Please, dear sweet Kuan Yin, Goddess of Love and all that is Good, do not let the white man suffer at the hands of the Lord Han Shen for what I am about to do. *Yesu*, take pity on me in my loneliness and despair.'

Szu-ma was frowning, looking down at her, for she had stopped climbing.

'Hurry!' he said angrily. 'In the name of the Buddha, move your bones!'

'So sorry!' she called up. 'All so sorry, dear Szu-ma, but cannot continue with you now.'

'You will do as you are told.'

'Forgive, please,' she said helplessly. 'Gave solemn word to stay with dog. Aubrey Paul, he say, watch over ol' boy.'

'He is not your master. No Chinese girl belongs to a barbarian. You have a new master now. Must do as he says.'

She nodded her head sadly. 'The Lord Han Shen, he say nothing at all. This my place—till Rayn, he all strong enough to walk again. You, most noble Szu-ma, must go see honourable lord. Tell him Sea Jade so sorry, but she gave word to barbarian to care for dog. Would be dishonourable to break word, and would bring everlasting shame upon Sea Jade's lowly head.'

He could have forced her to go with him. It would have been simplicity itself to fetch her and throw her bodily on Dancing Snow's back, but Szu-ma hesitated. There was something about the girl's expression, a quiet dignity that seemed misplaced. And, too, his master's rapid despatch of the two enemies, the look in his eyes as he had stared at the girl, made Szu-ma unsure about man-handling her.

'Forgive, please,' Sea Jade pleaded again. 'All my fault. Tell lord and master, all my own lowly and despicable fault.'

Defeated, Szu-ma turned away from her, knowing that, by leaving her, it could well mean a death-sentence placed on his own head. He must therefore continue the journey at the snail's pace set by Sea Jade and the dog.

Wang Ch'ung, who had been waiting near the gates of the house, grinned as Dark Messenger raced towards him. Han Shen was clearly in a mood as black as the hairs on his horse's back. Once through the gates, he dismounted with one supple movement, and a stable coolie ran forward to take the animal. Han Shen gave no sign that he had seen his friend waiting for him.

'Lord,' Wang Ch'ung said smoothly, 'I welcome your return.'

'*Hai!*'

'May speak?' Because he was privileged above all others, Wang Ch'ung fell easily into step at his master's side.

'If you must,' Han Shen said coldly, and narrowed his eyes against the glare of light, his expression not auguring well for those in his path.

'When anger is unfair, is misplaced.' Wang Ch'ung

was unperturbed. 'Own humble self must speak. Must make position clear. Was not girl's fault!'

'Nevertheless,' Han Shen's voice was like a strand of cold steel cutting the air, 'I intend to have her punished. She is disobedient.'

'She obeyed! She gave word to barbarian. Is my humble opinion that even lowly peasant girls do not wish to lose face.'

'From what I saw, the dog is a lost cause. And as for Szu-ma, he should have known better. I found it unseemly to see one of my best men acting like a fisherman's cormorant—collared and held by a string.'

Wang Ch'ung's grin widened at that, and he replied easily, 'Szu-ma is young and impressionable. Later on, he will have a quiver full of women and know how to keep them in line. The women in Great Warrior's house bend like the willow before him—and to his son out of courtesy. However, I believe that Szu-ma is finding that the young girl with him now is a very different kettle of fish.'

'How so?' Han Shen drawled.

Wang Ch'ung, who found most things on earth 'disgusting', who enjoyed being vulgar, who had a ready sense of humour, and who could and did become a killer when necessary, had the temerity to slap his thigh with delight and openly question his lord's power of observation. 'You mean,' he teased, 'that you have not seen the girl? Have not realised that she is the loveliest flower on this earth? That her eyes are the most wondrous, her lips . . .'

'She is disobedient!'

'She has come to love that disgusting flea-bag, my friend! She even sneaked out of the inn when it was dark and went to rescue it. I heard this from the whining old goat who was carrying on about feeding an extra mouth.'

'She went out alone at night?' Han Shen was frowning and seemed more angry. 'She could have been killed—or worse.'

'Ah so! The innkeeper made so much fuss about the animal that I said he could have it—rather than throw good money away to pay for its keep. The girl did not know. When she did, she threw herself off Mountain Arrow's back and ran like the wind to defend the dog, caring nothing about the cleaver the man had in his hand.

Han Shen's eyes narrowed.

'Then she is mad as well as self-willed!'

'Perhaps, but . . .' Wang Ch'ung was suddenly thoughtful. 'Now I come to think of it, when she leapt off Mountain Arrow, she knew what she was doing. By the gods, she knows a great deal about riding, my friend! She is something of a mystery, eh?'

'You say she actually loves the dog?' Han Shen's tone was coldly disbelieving.

'Why else should she risk so much on its behalf? She called it "Ol'—boy".'

'Perhaps it is the Englishman . . .'

'How so?' Wang Ch'ung raised his brows. 'You and I know that he has been unconscious, or partly so, all the time she had known him. We also know the truth about how she came to be at the Iris Pool in the first place. No, she has taken to the dog. I must admit it seems a loyal and courageous beast. In spite of its injuries, it was still trying to follow her.'

Han Shen was now puzzled rather than angry. 'I wonder,' he said slowly, 'whether the palace messenger told us the whole truth? A peasant girl, they said, sent along to escort a missionary to the House of the Golden Lilies. We were ordered to help in any way that we could.'

'The plan was then changed! Now girl and barbarian are no concern of ours. This was most explicit message,' Wang Ch'ung reminded him. 'Should not even think of bringing either of them here to your noble house.'

'You have numerous friends and relatives who can help.' Han Shen was not listening to the warning. 'I want to know all about that girl. She has an air about her that is hard to define. She wishes me to believe her to be a lowly person, so . . . Even if she turns out to be a princess, she is to be treated as nothing but a peasant. It will be interesting to see how she gets on. It shall be between us, eh, Ch'ung?'

'*Hai!* And what about now?'

'Let her continue her walk,' Han Shen ordered, and allowed himself to smile in a tight, superior way. 'It will do her good.'

'And the barbarian?'

'Is to have the best possible care. He interests me, I don't know why. Perhaps it will be a good idea to familiarise ourselves with the mission house, too. I would like to know what goes on there. Barbarians are inexplicable. Their ways bring puzzlement, their beliefs are obscure. I find it of some interest now to wonder what they are doing at the mission. To find out if they know and are concerned about the fate of one of their kind.'

'Officially, you are to leave well alone. Could cause much trouble should you disobey.'

Han Shen ignored his friend yet again. He was beginning to feel an interest in all matters appertaining to the girl—who intrigued him more than he cared to admit, even to himself.

He found himself growing fascinated with the idea of seeing her proposed destination. The Mission House of the Golden Lilies did not sound too grand a place. Worse, it was all but on top of Peking. Han Shen found his own lands far superior. They did not belong to the plain, but edged it, and rose with quiet magnificence to the hills. Hills that, in turn, gave way to the mountains, the abode of Buddha's temple and his yellow-gowned priests. Yes, Han Shen had a deep and abiding love for his land, and an affection for his people. But, for all that, he would go to the mission. However, there was no immediate hurry, he decided. The visit could take place later. For now, he was curious to see what the peasant girl would do next. He would allow things to take their course. He would give orders that the girl be put to work in the women's part of the house. The dog must be cared for and taken to its master.

Han Shen felt further curiosity as he thought of the barbarian. The man's physical health had improved already. Bathed and with good food inside him, he had quickly begun to pick up. The gash on his head was knitting nicely. Even so, he was in pain, his eyes were dazed, and he seemed to have difficulty in knowing who he was. The physicians had nodded their heads and fed him potions and pills. Had talked about 'Bruising of Brain' and 'Need of Healing of Time', of amnesia that had been brought about through 'Blow of Evil' and Shock.

In a while, if no improvement occurred, Han Shen thought, he would send the girl to the barbarian and see what she could do. In the meantime, she had a lesson about obedience to learn, and first things must be first.

A messenger came running up.

'What is it?' Han Shen asked.

'Honourable lord, the girl with Lord Szu-ma has been seen. She still walks with dog, their progress is slow. Their arrival will not be for some little time.'

'Then you must wait.' Han Shen showed his displeasure. 'But, first, go and tell Madam Night Bird how it is. It is impossible for me to understand why all this time has been wasted. This situation angers me.' He strode away with Wang Ch'ung doggedly walking at his side. 'We will play cards,' Han Shen said abruptly. 'And gamble our time away in much pleasure. We will give that girl no further thought. She shall be placed in Night Bird's care, and that will be an end to it.'

'Poor little child!' Wang Ch'ung replied. 'I would not put a goat in care of that old woman.'

'That is enough!' Han Shen snapped. 'Subject is closed.'

CHAPTER FIVE

THE SETTING SUN'S last defiance had left raging red ribbons flying behind it in the sky. The women's court-yard in the House of Han was large, paved and beautiful. Surrounded by an ornamental wall, graced by a Moon Gate of exquisite design, it was gracious, spacious and held trees, shrubs and flowers.

It was timeless in the courtyard, Sea Jade thought. Ageless! The shadows under the wall and the trees seemed secretive. The night breeze kissing against slivers of crystal carried the soul music of tiny bells. She had no music. They had taken her flute away. Her tears made blurred fruits of the coloured lanterns hanging in the branches, and there was a poignancy in the sleepy melodies whistled by the birds. The high curving cry of an unseen peacock held an eeriness in its sound, and she shivered at the call. She wished she was at the Golden Lilies Mission, anywhere but here!

Never had she felt so lost and alone. Even the Inn of Great Security and Content had been noisy with animals and the vulgarity of drunken carters' songs. But here, in the women's courtyard of the House of Han, there was a stifling sense of apartness. It came to her again, that Chinese concubines and wives were like slaves. Her mind darted back to the first sight of the place. How abruptly the hills had leapt up from the edge of the plain, and on the brow of one hill, like a beacon proclaiming the presence of man, a large, singularly magnificent Chinese house. Even higher, before the mountains, a temple built to the love of Buddha stood like a reminder of faith.

Sea Jade trembled with humiliation as she thought of the horrible Madam Night Bird. The degradation of her own arrival in Lord Han Shen's home. How relieved Szu-ma had seemed as he had handed her over to the obsequious servant, who had quite clearly been expecting her for a very long time.

She had been taken quickly to the women who had been amusing themselves in the tea-house. Everyone had stopped speaking at her entrance, and the only sound then had been the chirping of linnets and the whirring of pretty silk and paper fans. Number One Lady, Madam Night Bird, was sitting on the highest chair. The ladies round her seemed very subdued.

'You have taken a long time to get here,' Night Bird said, and her voice, like her small eyes, was cold and hard.

Everything about Night Bird made Sea Jade's heart take a leap down to her feet. The woman's face was cruel and lined, in spite of her make-up. Her nails were three inches long, which showed how high a personage she was. Her black silk clothes bore the same hallmark. They were embroidered richly with bands of silver, red and gold. Silver, red and gold ornaments also adorned her greying hair. Night Bird was well named: she had a stiff, predatory air. Her feet were only four inches long, but her 'lilies' did not imprison her. Servants were there at all times to help her to move from place to place. It was quite clear that Madam Night Bird ruled the women with a rod of iron.

Sea Jade waited, after her first polite kowtow. Her head was bowed, her eyes fixed firmly on the ground. She looked the epitome of obedience, but deep down a little spark of anger was beginning to glow. She was the Honourable Ling Sea Jade, who had managed to get her own way with men. She would not let this hateful old woman over-rule her now!

'It is Lord Han Shen's wish that you make yourself useful here,' Night Bird said coldly. 'You will be quick and obedient. You will remain silent at all times. You will accept that, should you fail in your duties, even for an instant, you will be whipped.'

Sea Jade had never been whipped in her life. Outrage shook her. She thought of Peach Velvet, the sweet, gentle Number One Lady in her father's house, and wanted to weep. She kept very quiet and still, waiting for what was next to come.

'You will attend the needs of Miss Beautiful Spring-time and Miss Summer Rain,' Night Bird said. 'But, ultimately, in all matters you are subject to my command. Do I make myself clear?'

'Honourable madam,' Sea Jade had whispered. 'There is some mistake. I have come here to care for the white barbarian. This "duty" was set for me by those high above. I am not a servant in this house.'

'You gave up your duty towards the Christian when you allowed him to arrive here unattended and half dead,' Night Bird replied. 'I have heard all about how, to undertake your duty, you forgot it and gave your attention to a dog!'

The word 'dog' was spat out in utmost contempt, and Sea Jade was thankful that Rayn has been given into the care of Honourable Horse Doctor. When Rayn's wounds had been seen to, he was to be taken directly to the Aubrey Paul. They had given her their word. She cast caution to the wind. She lifted her head and looked straight into Night Bird's black eyes.

'Forgive me, honourable lady, but I must explain. I gave solemn oath to the mission man, to care for dog. He say, "Look after Rayn. He good ol' boy." I kept word. I am not a servant in this house.'

'You are what I say you are. No more, no less.'

'Forgive, please,' Sea Jade had stammered, conscious that by daring to argue she had made the ladies murmur and flutter their fans. 'But I must . . . I wish to speak personally to the Lord Han Shen.'

This was so startling, so shocking, that the ladies gasped. No one had ever dared to speak back to Night

Bird before, let alone seek to go over her head and ask to
see the master of the house!

Night Bird opened her snapping jet-bead eyes very
wide, and Sea Jade knew that she had made an implacable enemy. Her heart was beating, her hands were
clammy. She was incapable of disobeying the hissed
command.

'Come here!'

She took the two steps necessary.

'Kowtow!'

She knelt humbly at the vicious old woman's feet.
Night Bird raised her slim bamboo cane and beat her
about the shoulders. It was a beating that Sea Jade found
painful—but, far worse, humiliating. With all her heart
and soul she wanted to jump up and pull the cane out of
those skinny, claw-like hands. She dared not. The
Dowager Empress had said that she must be a peasant in
look, thought, word and deed. No matter that the order
had been rescinded, she had given her word. She would
therefore play her part until the gods saw fit to place her
once again safely in her father's house. She gritted her
teeth and did not cry out. She would never give the
woman that satisfaction!

When the beating was over, Night Bird said in a bright
voice, 'You will now go to Well of Happiness and
meditate on sin of disobedience. Since you prefer the
company of dogs, you will stay outside like a dog. You
may not even shelter in the servants' quarters at night.'

Sea Jade had been taken to the women's courtyard
by a skinny, trembling little girl-servant, who could
have been no more than seven years old. The child left
her, melting away nervously. Not a word had been
said.

All that had happened some hours ago. Sea Jade had
quietly waited. And in her mind she was missing the
comfort and love she had felt she had seen—in the eyes
of the black and yellow dog.

*   *   *

Rayn sat patiently by the bed on which Paul lay. There was neither recognition nor feeling reaching out to him from his master, who had been drugged in order to ease his pain. A Chinese doctor came to the bedside again, with him the revered mystic and fortune-teller. The wise man, thin-bearded, very old and hardly of this world, looked at Rayn and gravely nodded his head.

'Is bad joss, him here,' he said in his thin, high voice. 'All bad joss. No good!'

Rayn was unceremoniously shooed away.

Sea Jade shivered. The night was cold. She was home-sick and hungry, and very tired. Try though she did, she could neither think nor plan. There was a numbness in her brain: a numbness as unbearable as the burning on her shoulders where her skin had been broken by the strokes of the cane. She felt isolated and without a friend in the world. Then suddenly, blessedly, a dark shadow seemed to fly through the air as it leapt through the Moon Gate.

Rayn went over to Sea Jade, his nose nudging her lovingly, a gentle tongue licking comfortingly at her face. Her arms went round his warm furry body, and she rested her cheek against him, her eyes bright with unshed tears.

'Good ol' boy!' she whispered. 'You came to me! Dear good ol' boy!' Suddenly the courtyard was a warm and friendly place. It was shelter, not like the harsh wilderness away from the Iris Pool. There were no rebels to bear down on one, wielding daggers and knives. No killers! She was safe in the ladies' Well of Happiness. She had a friend, and she was the Miss Ling Sea Jade, honourable member of her father's house. The daughter of the honourable Ling Fu could never be cowed by a spiteful old woman, she thought. There was more to the Lings than that!

She hugged Rayn, her confidence restored. She was

unaware that Night Bird, having had a quiet conversation with a woman belonging to Wang Ch'ung, had a rapid change of plan. The first thing Sea Jade knew was that a little girl-servant came scurrying out with a dish of rice and the message that she might now take shelter in the servants' quarters.

Sea Jade replied with a quiet dignity, 'Please thank Madam Night Bird for the rice. I am grateful for it. But I will stay here.

'Oh—oh!' The little girl's eyes were wide in her face. 'Must do as told. Is order!'

'I will stay here—with my friend,' Sea Jade said calmly. 'I am quite sure that Ol' Boy would not be allowed anywhere near Night Bird's part of the house.'

'You will be whipped again!' The child was near to tears.

'Is not so bad,' Sea Jade replied, then smiled, and said again firmly, 'Is not so bad!'

'You are very brave!'

'I am far from that. Tell me, what do they call you?'

'Dark Pebble,' the child replied gravely. 'I am dull like dark pebble. I am not very bright.'

'Really? You do not look dull to me, and so that is silly thing to say.' Sea Jade's smile then was wide and warm and wonderful. 'I like dark pebbles very much.'

'They not pretty. Of no consequence.'

'Of great consequence!' Sea Jade's tone was most decided. 'They shine, and are beautiful when they are kissed by the sparkling waters of a clear stream. You will shine like a star and be very beautiful when you are surrounded by love.'

'No one loves Dark Pebble,' the child said wistfully.

'I love you,' Sea Jade replied. 'I love you very much, Dark Pebble, because you brought me food and because, when you thought I might be whipped, your heart was so sad. You all same happy now, little girl?'

'I love you!' Dark Pebble whispered passionately and ran away, back to the house.

There were no chopsticks, so Sea Jade ate with her fingers, rolling the cooked rice into small mouth-sized balls. These she shared with Rayn. They slept together, she and the large dog, gaining comfort and warmth from each other. At dawn, when he could have left her, Rayn stayed.

Dark Pebble, risking punishment, crept out to tell her, 'Madam Night Bird, she say you beneath contempt. You suffer. You stay here. You stay here allee time. You disobey, she lose face.'

'I must find a way to speak to the Lord Han Shen. I must!'

'He not long here,' Dark Pebble said frantically. 'He all leave in two-three days. He go see white missionary place. Barbarian doctor, he look-see barbarian man! Hear much talkee-talk. Lord Han Shen bring danger to this place. The Lord Han Shen go own way. Go against court! Madam Night Bird, she angry with lord. She say he get us all killed!'

'That only means that Madam Night Bird is afraid for herself,' Sea Jade observed comfortingly, 'Do not think about all scary things. Think of nice times. Happy times, eh?'

'All very proper to have happy times,' Dark Pebble said. 'Is nice like sunshine! I am too afraid of this day, that day. Allee time I get in disgrace. Forget duties, get cane.' She looked very mournful as she added, 'Get cane allee time.'

She turned then and ran swiftly back to the servants' quarters. Thin, frail, a poor little waif.

'When I leave this forbidding place, Ol' Boy,' Sea Jade whispered to Rayn, 'we will take little child with us. We will make her sparkle like a little star. Maybe, one day, we find her a nice husband. One as good and fine as honourable father will find for me one day.'

The thought shook her and she tried to forget it, but the idea that had leapt unbidden into her mind refused to go away. Sea Jade found herself wondering about the husband her father would choose for her, all in good time. Would he be handsome and young, or old, wise and revered? How would it feel—to be a man's Within One? How would she react to the making of love? What did it matter? It would be a small price to pay, to be protected and safe. Her hand flew to her lips and she now felt very shy at her thoughts. She hoped very much that she would like and respect her husband. If the gods were kind, she might even learn to love him one day. How nice that would be. The honourable Ling Fu had always said that he would choose her lord and master with great care. He had been very firm about that. 'He must be the right one for you, my child,' he had said to her one day. 'But there is no hurry. To lose you will make me sad.'

What kind of man would be the right one? She remembered the fierce and noble Han Shen, and her heart raced. But he was as high above her as the stars. An exalted, regal man, and she? She was a peasant girl in his eyes. She hastily pushed the thought of Han Shen away, but somehow she felt that he would always be there—strong, very masculine, a dominating figure at the back of her mind. Then her heart melted as she pictured the barbarian. How the sunlight had made his hair look like gold. His eyes, that were as blue as the summer sky. He was foreign and beautiful, like a strange god carved from ivory. He would find loving a warm and gentle thing, almost spiritual, perhaps. Did the English make love like Chinamen did? She blushed at the idea, and went on to wonder whether all men were formed in the same way. How achingly beautiful it would be, she thought, to be loved by the white barbarian.

She was left alone all that day. In the early evening, when the shadows fell, Dark Pebble came through the Moon Gate again, with a tray on which was set a plate of pastry fingers and a little dish of tea.

'Honourable Beautiful Springtime and also Summer Rain sent this,' she explained. 'They say eat and drink, chop chop. Allee very bad for them if Night Bird find out.'

'They are kind!' Sea Jade's eyes sparkled with tears; they were concerned about her. They were not all like evil old Night Bird, after all.

'They good. Good even to own lowly self,' Dark Pebble explained. 'They say you either very brave or stupid to defy Madam Night Bird, who is fierce and all-powerful round here. She—they say—she know the Lord Han Shen all the days of his life. Hide tray! Hide dish! Must go!'

'The Lord Han Shen, how . . .'

'He keep to himself in own part of house. Is true what I heard. They say that honourable lord is thinking of going to mission house. Wants white man to have comfort of seeing own kind . . . Hide tray!' Dark Pebble was away again, running and afraid, on her small, unbound feet.

Sea Jade found herself smiling—the world was getting rosier all the time. She had friends. With a little good joss on her side, perhaps she could be free of the House of Han quite soon. Missionaries coming here would effectively free her from any promises she had made to herself. She must begin to make plans for her escape.

She was thoroughly enjoying the thin golden-brown pastry fingers that had been deep fried. They were flavoured with cinnamon, and were crispy and sweet. Rayn nudged her hand with his nose and looked up at her with bright expectant eyes.

'You getting better,' she told him. 'Horse doctor's ointment good. Make you old self. What is more, Ol' Boy, you getting greedy!'

She handed him a piece of pastry, which was disposed of at a gulp. Rayn wagged his tail and waited eagerly for more. With infinite love and care, Sea Jade began to feed him.

The next morning her tasks began. She was allotted

everything that was low and menial. She was kept scurrying backwards and forwards by an impatient Madam Night Bird who was never satisfied.

Rayn was left to himself outside, but he was fed, and given water to drink. Night Bird was far more lenient than she would have liked to have been. But one of Wang Ch'ung's women had whispered in her ear, 'Is believed lord master, he likee girl!'

Out of sheer hatefulness Madam Night Bird found it very necessary to call the peasant girl many times, and a new chore was found especially for her. It was Sea Jade's job to bend her back so that Honourable Lady could use her as a step up to the high chair. It was a cold, calculated, indignity. It had not even been Dark Pebble's duty before.

Sea Jade begged only once more for a privilege. She kowtowed before the older woman, and entreated, 'Honourable First Lady, may I please visit the white man to see how he is?'

'By all accounts, he lives,' Night Bird said harshly. 'Which is a great pity, I think.'

'Honourable Number One,' Sea Jade whispered desperately. 'May own humble self have permission to approach the lord?'

'Arrogant nothing!' The cane fell across Sea Jade's shoulders three spiteful times. 'The master can have no time for a creature as low as you. How dare you presume even to address me! I am your superior, and you are less than the dirt at my feet.'

Beautiful Springtime and Summer Rain, helpless, watched with sad eyes.

Han Shen made no enquiries about the mysterious girl, who was now learning the lesson of abject obedience in his house. He could not quite understand why she was always there at the back of his mind. Why he had been so angry when she had clapped her hands and laughed so freely and joyously up into Szu-ma's face? Why he had wanted to whip her because she had been so unwilling to arrive at his house?

It came to him to wonder what her life would be, had it worked out as the Dowager Empress had planned. Would she have been better off with the barbarians? Would they have accepted her? They would, most certainly, never have looked on her as one of themselves.

The white Christian now under his roof was proving to be an enigma. He had not improved mentally, though he was now physically very well. Did the girl care for him? Was that what she wanted? To be used like a Flower Boat girl, then to be abandoned, perhaps? His lips curled as he thought, that was not *their* way. They were Christians.

Ha! He had heard quite a lot about the visiting male white Christians, how they treated the women of this land. Oh yes, he could tell a tale or two. Celestials were more honourable by far—and not hypocritical like the whites.

Two more days went by, and everything remained the same. Han Shen decided that the time to visit the Mission House of the Golden Lilies had arrived. The whole situation was puzzling, irritating, and he had to do something to banish the peasant from his thoughts. He gave instructions, and made his preparations to leave. He would call for the girl—whose name was Sea Jade—on his return. Then she would see how graciously he could relent!

He called Szu-ma and some of his men, and they set out. Sea Jade, Han Shen was thinking. A pretty name, clear, cool and lovely—like the girl herself.

Christina was now resigned to Dr Kingsleigh's presence in the mission. There had been no news about Paul Aubrey, or of Li, her father's faithful servant and friend, who had left his master and gone to find someone who could give the beloved Reverend final spiritual blessings and help.

Once the doctor had made his dramatic appearance into her life, he had taken things over completely. He was quick, crisp and methodical. He had a system, and it worked. So far as his patients were concerned, he was a dedicated man. He could be ruthless—and was, until he got his own way. He was either loved or loathed, and Christina loathed him.

She saw very little of him. When they met at meal-times, he was studiously polite, but distant. When she went to the surgery part of the house, he would give her the briefest of instructions as to what she must do. She would flare up at him, but he would grin in his devilish way and leave her to cope with mountains of work. He had tireless energy himself and expected an all-out effort from those around him. Woe betide anyone attempting to shirk! Unwillingly, Christina had to admit to admiring him.

These days, there seemed to be a steady stream of Chinese Christians coming through the gates, since the hostilities towards them were growing ever more open and pronounced. The news was getting unbearable. It seemed that, now, whole families were being hacked down.

Christina, engrossed in her work, glad that she was helping, sure that her father would have been proud of her, pressed on. She struggled at setting up classes for women with the help of the books she had. Her pupils were a mere handful of dedicated ladies, quite charming, rather shy and anxious to learn. Through all this Christina had Lotus's help, and it was Lotus's calm eyes and warm smile that gave her courage and strength.

Lotus was a Christian, but there were also many Chinese deities in which she believed and perhaps was even a little afraid of. But the earthly god she had now come to cherish—and for whom she would lay down her life—was Dr Alan Kingsleigh.

'Such worship of a man, Lotus!' Christina said exasperatedly after one particularly wearisome day. 'Yet only this morning he was raging at you and carrying on like a bear with a sore head.'

'Was sad.' There was understanding in Lotus's eyes. 'Is because his heart cries that his tongue holds the sharpness of a knife.'

'Why was he sad? I was not aware that he was capable of such human feeling,' Christina replied pithily.

'A child died. He was angry, he not in time. He feel very bad about this. He say . . .'

'Children seem to die very easily out here, Lotus.' Christina's voice was bleak with regret. 'How can they survive against all but impossible odds? Like being sold into what amounts to slavery for a few pence? Like being an abandoned and unwanted little girl left to die, afraid and alone, in the street?'

'Childs who died here was muchee wanted. He a Number One Son! Father cry out against Fate.'

'Then it did not help the mother to be shouted at by the doctor, and . . .'

'Childs would have lived if mother had brought him here sooner.'

'Even so, he nearly snapped the poor woman's head off, and she was breaking her heart.' Christina's eyes flashed. 'Men!'

'Men cannot weep, we women can. Honourable doctor, he hides compassion beneath surface of stone. This lowly self understands simple truth. The louder the doctor shouts, the greater he cares.'

'He is hard and ruthless. The kind of man I despise,' she said unconvincingly. Lotus smiled.

'Not muchee good to despise! Honourable father, he say, love everyone.'

'I know.' Christina felt perilously near to tears. 'No one can ever come up to him, not now or ever.'

There came a commotion outside, and Christina went to the window and looked towards the gates. A man on horseback was riding proudly towards the mission building—and what a man! He sat, tall and regal in the

silver-tassel-decorated saddle. He was dressed in a long
scarlet silk tunic that was thickly embroidered with gold.
His trousers were black, as were his white-soled shoes.
His face was refined, noble-looking and handsome. His
long hair was pulled severely back from his face. Everything about him was magnificent, from the jewelled
sword hanging at his side to the peacock-plume in his
black and gold cap. Behind him came a bevy of mounted
men wearing dark and light blue.

Christina gasped, while Lotus was almost rigid with
delighted shock. A mandarin of very high class and
distinction! For, as he turned to give an order to his men,
they saw the coral button at the back of his cap, and the
feather, too.

Mandarins, Christina well knew, were the most important people in China. If he wore a gilt button on his
cap, he belonged to the lowest rank, if the button was
glass, he was much better class. The really important
mandarins wore coral buttons. If one also wore a
peacock's feather at the back of his cap, then you knew
he was in special favour with the throne.

What Christina did not know was that by openly
associating with the barbarians' Christian Mission
House, Han Shen was endangering not only his rank,
but also that of all of the members of his house—and
even his own life.

'I am Han Shen,' he proclaimed with quiet dignity. 'I
have come to see Number One Personage here.'

Wide-eyed and in an ecstacy of awe, young Wu, who
had magically appeared by the gates at that precise
moment, scuttled away.

Christina swiftly smoothed her hair, then went outside
to greet the visitor. When she came to a halt before him,
she made a polite, ceremonial kowtow.

'Welcome to the Golden Lilies Mission House, my
lord.'

Han Shen looked into a pair of large blue eyes that
were the colour of the flowers at the Iris Pool. His

haughty expression did not alter, but a slight rising of his right brow gave his surprise away. He thought the barbarian girl strange, and yet rather lovely. He did not think her nose too long, her body ugly, or her feet too big. He accepted the thought, then his gaze went away, over the white girl's shoulder, to the tall, scowling barbarian heading towards him.

Alan Kingsleigh stopped beside Christina. He did not bother to be polite.

'You wanted to see me?' he asked. 'Couldn't it have waited at all? Oh hell!' He turned exasperatedly towards Christina. 'You know the lingo a darned sight better than I. Find out exactly what he wants. If it's not important, tell him I'll speak to him later. I have patients waiting for me.'

Christina smiled up at Han Shen in her warm, friendly way, and said, 'Please forgive Dr Kingsleigh's haste. He has many sick people to attend to, and . . .'

'Sick?' Han Shen's tone was cold. 'The white people are sick?'

'No. Dr Kingsleigh is looking after a group of near-starving Chinese Christians who arrived early today. There is a little boy who is very ill, and . . .' She shrugged expressively.

'I understand,' Han Shen said stiffly. 'What I have to say will not take long. Tell the doctor that I have in my house a certain white man who was set upon on his way here. I believe he is known as Aubrey Paul?'

'Oh!' Christina swung round to Dr Kingsleigh. 'Doctor, the Lord Han Shen has Mr Aubrey in his house!' She turned back to the visitor. 'Lord, you say that he was set upon? He is hurt?'

'Very badly. I believe a man answering to the name of Li was travelling with him? Li is with his honourable ancestors now.'

'Oh!' Christina gasped and reeled back, shocked and impossibly sad.

'What is it?' Dr Kingsleigh snapped.

'Li,' she wept. 'Our sweet darling old Li has been killed, and—and Mr Aubrey is hurt very badly. Dear heaven, has the whole world gone mad?'

'No—only China,' he replied sourly. 'Ask what injuries Aubrey has sustained.'

Christina looked to Han Shen, who had clearly understood. He was sitting there, his thoughts hidden behind an inscrutable face. Here was a man who would never suffer fools gladly. Perhaps he believed, as did many of his kind, that white people were all upstarts and fools.

'I take opportunity,' Han Shen said haughtily, 'to point out that we have our own physicians, some of whom are considered to be quite brilliant in their field. As to the honourable doctor's question, the missionary has head wounds, is conscious only some of the time, but is physically well, owing to the ceaseless devotion of lowly Chinese peasant girl.'

Kingsleigh had the grace to look ashamed. 'Forgive me.' His apology was swift and sincere. 'I meant no disrespect, but it's like trying to hold back the sea round here. It was good of you to take in one of our kind, particularly with the situation as it is now. As for putting yourself out in coming here like this, I'm sure that we'll be eternally grateful.'

'Gratitude is unnecessary. The barbarian is welcome in my humble abode. However . . .' Piercing dark eyes flicked towards Christina. 'The missionary needs a nurse who is of own race. Has Chinese girl fussing round him, but needs English lady most.'

'Sorry. No,' Kingsleigh said flatly.

Han Shen managed to look even more regal and superior as he stared down from Dark Messenger's back. 'Forgive, please,' he said calmly. 'Would humbly point out that great House of Han is an honourable establishment. I must also say that if own lowly self desired a white woman, would neither beg nor ask. Would take!'

'Exactly!' Kingsleigh snapped.

Han Shen permitted himself a cool, superior smile, but his eyes remained oblique. 'Was thinking that as my guest is Christian, as Christians yourselves, you would recognise his need! However . . .'

He let the rest of his sentence hang in mid-air, the silence more stinging than any amount of accusing words.

Christina stepped forward impulsively. 'Lord Han Shen,' she said quickly. 'You have looked after the man who is to take over my late father's position. We are all humbly grateful, and aware that you are a man of compassion. I shall consider it an honour to help to look after Mr Aubrey—with your permission, of course.'

'Don't be foolish!' Kingsleigh snapped. 'You don't know what you could be walking into. You only have this man's word; and, what is more, it's my opinion that your services are needed here.'

Christina's cheeks glowed with embarrassed anger. She did not look at him. How could he? How dared anyone on this earth be as rude, as discourteous, as he? And when this proud and handsome man had come personally to ask for help, too! Alan Kingsleigh did not seem to have a sensitive bone in his body. He was rough and hard, and getting to be unendurable. She stared gravely up into Han Shen's inscrutable face. 'I will go with you,' she said. 'It is my duty.'

Defeated, his face dark with anger, Alan Kingsleigh stepped back, then looked surprised, because Han Shen said, 'Young missee very necessary to well-being of missionary. Her delicate air, most soothing to his soul.' His dark eyes left Christina and returned to the doctor. 'However, is own opinion that white doctor also come to House of Han. Then he will personally judge health of missionary. Perhaps even suggest further treatment? Will at least settle own mind that Englishman is receiving adequate care?'

'Thank you,' he replied. 'I would like to do just that.'

For the second time during the last few minutes,

Christina felt like hitting him. And yet . . . It came to her that he was actually trying to defend her in his own irritable way. He did not like the idea of her going off with Han Shen. It was absurd of him, and sometimes he made her almost too furious to be true, yet . . . it was rather comforting to have someone like him on her side. Yes, even if he was only acting out of some kind of code of honour, his air of protection made her feel—safe!

Her own thoughts confused her, and she tried to brush them away.

CHAPTER SIX

HAN SHEN GRACIOUSLY accepted the hospitality offered. He walked round the mission, saw the living arrangements that had been made for the homeless poor, and saw the medical department, set in the second half of the house. He was aware that the Chinese people here were well cared for and happy. A Buddhist himself, he nevertheless accepted that the Rice Christians were at least devout. He felt an unwilling admiration for the English doctor, who was a dedicated, but evil-tempered, man.

He enjoyed a meal, humble but wholesome, prepared by a nervous Lotus, who was all fingers and thumbs before such a great man. He waited patiently while Christina Morrow and the barbarian doctor packed their bags and made ready to leave. Lotus was left in charge of the women, and Li's grieving Number One Son, Han, was to take over the rest. Christina and the doctor expected to return to the mission, with Paul, within the next three days.

It would be quite an adventure, Christina thought—if they were not set on by bands of Boxers, of course. She was quite at ease when Dr Kingsleigh arranged that she should not travel by rickshaw, but on a rather frisky little grey horse he had acquired for her. She could ride quite well, and she fell in love with her mount at first sight. 'Her name is Echo,' he said. 'I was thinking of buying her for myself. If you like her, she's yours.'

'Oh!' Christina breathed, and her smile was so wonderful that he felt a moment of startled surprise. 'I adore her. I really do!'

They set out . . .

*   *   *

Han Shen was glad that the mission was behind them. It was too near Peking, which was dirty and overcrowded, a sink of iniquity. He could almost feel the panting sighs of a million people. He thought of the city streets. Of how hot winds would swirl the rubbish round in the gutters. How sheets of grit and dust would cover the coolies as they slept dreamlessly, swathed in old rags, paper . . . anything. They huddled like so many stick-thin toys as they sought forgetfulness, lying among the litter on the ground.

And yet even the coolies were more content than he at this precise moment. He felt angry and unsettled, yet hardly knew why. He was not happy away from his own environment, well to the north, by the old yellow hills. Even more irritating, he could not get one small, infinitely lovely, girl out of his mind.

It had been a mistake to overlook the dog. She cared for the creature, Wang Ch'ung had said. He hoped devoutly that she did not also care for the white man. Chinese girls and barbarians could never mix, never be right, he thought coldly. He would never let it come to that, nor would the girl's people, whoever they were. Still, there would be no mystery about her soon. Wang Ch'ung's people were spread far and wide and had eyes and ears everywhere. They would soon meet with good knowledge that would, in turn, come back to him. He would consider his own actions from there on. He urged Dark Messenger forward. Proud and superior, he did not wish to mingle with the white people at his back. Again his mind returned to Sea Jade.

Christina, at ease on the jaunty little mare, was very aware of the doctor riding at her side. She felt unsure of him and of his attitudes. How could she come to terms with a man who ranted and raved and went about looking like a bear with a sore head? Yet when it boiled down to caring and healing, he became gentleness itself. Quite clearly, he had no time for her, and she thought that if Lotus were with them, or even young Wu, they

could have a laugh and a talk. She was wishing that the
doctor would show at least a little appreciation of
herself.

Behind them, Han Shen's men, wary, rode on guard,
a clear indication that these were troubled times.

The sun was far into the western sky before Han Shen
called a halt. They had reached the vicinity of Bright
Water Stream. Even though he would have liked to have
gone on, Han Shen knew that he could not expect the
young white woman to ride further that day. The men
made camp while Han Shen sat in splendid isolation.
Having fed and watered their horses, Christina and Han
went over to the large thorn-fire the Chinese had made.
Food was being prepared: rice, vegetables, meat and
fruit. Christina offered to help, but the cooks, stony-
faced, turned her down. Spurned, she walked away.

Dr Kingsleigh sprawled on the ground, near the fire,
quite at home. Christina hesitated, then sat herself down
beside him. The food smelled good and appetising, and
she felt hungry in spite of her aching bones.

'I'm starving,' she said, her tone so aggrieved that the
man at her side threw back his head and laughed.

For the first time since she had known him, the doctor
had laughed outright. Laughter suited him, Christina
decided. He had nice teeth, strong and even, and his
mouth became younger when not so determined and
hard. There were attractive crinkles round his eyes that
softened the lines on his face. She smiled wryly.

'Doctor,' she said. 'What is it that's so funny?'

'You!'

'I'm not sure I understand . . .'

'And that's the real peach of it, you honestly don't
know! Here you are, in a camp of Chinese people, and at
the mercy of their chief. We English are loathed and
detested. Christians are being mown down everywhere.
The Boxers are rampaging quite openly, and I swear
they have the blessing of those on high. We could be set
upon at any moment—by this lot here, or even by

murderous swine skulking somewhere out of sight—and you're concerned only about that flat and beautiful little stomach of yours!'

She chuckled softly and looked curiously at his brown profile, at the amusement deep in his eyes. He was leaning back, relaxed, happy to tease her and wait for her to retort as she usually did, but she hesitated. She sensed something of the deep loneliness of the man, and a turbulence inside him. She found that she wanted to know more about him and, because he was suddenly approachable, she dared to ask, 'Why did they make you leave India?'

'You really want to know?' He was still smiling, and she felt relief. He could quite easily have become the stiff, angry stranger again.

'Yes,' she replied quietly. 'I do.'

'Very well, here it is, straight from the horse's mouth. There was a lady, a sweet and lovely person.' His face was twisted with sarcasm as he said that. 'I was in love with her. On her side, she said she was in love with me, that her husband was too old and too authoritative, and that he had no time for her. She was playing a little game, of course.'

'What happened?'

'The world fell in, that's what happened. The husband was a nice chap, and rich. He was not all that old, either, but rather more concerned with running his plantation than amusing his bored wife. When he found out about her affair with me he told her to pack her bags. So . . .' He paused and looked at Christina, and she could almost feel his sizzling contempt. 'So to keep her nice home and her rich husband, she lied. She accused me of rape.'

'Oh!'

'Yes, exactly. Thank God, the truth came out, all of it. It seems the lady had been in love once or twice before. There is a great deal of gossip in India, you know. The only chaps who never knew what a peach she was were her husband—and I. I was cleared, absolutely, but I had become an embarrassment. So—goodbye India, hello China, and here we jolly well are.'

'And you're hating every minute of it?'

'Now now. I'm over it all now. Too much to do here; and, at least,' he smiled bleakly, 'the problems are somewhat different, wouldn't you say?'

'I'm sorry,' she said quietly. 'About your trouble out there, I mean. It must have been very difficult for you.'

'My pride took a blow, my work came to a halt, but I am still kicking and breathing. I feel angry, though. Not because of her, but because of me. I was a fool, a damned stupid fool, but I've learned my lesson now.'

'And you'll never trust a woman again, is that it?'

'Exactly.'

'Will you ever go back?'

'That, my dear Miss Morrow, is in the lap of the gods and no concern of yours. Now tell me, what about you?'

'My life is here. I love this land and the people.'

'Murderers? You actually like the celestials?'

'Yes, I do,' she said firmly. 'And only someone with a closed mind could look at a whole race of people and see them as all the same. Every country has its good, its bad, and its ordinary. I'm one of England's ordinarys, and quite content about it.'

He was looking at her now, really looking at her, and she felt herself going pink to the roots of her hair.

'You're not so everyday,' he told her. 'In fact, I'd say quite the reverse. Lord! When are they going to dish up the food?'

At that moment one of Han Shen's men came up and kowtowed before them, saying, 'The lord master Han Shen sends you felicitations. He say please to honour him with your august company.'

'How nice! Thank you,' Christina replied, while the doctor unwound his tall body and sprang to his feet to help her up.

The meal was delicious. Lots of little dishes of savouries and a large communal bowl of rice. They were waited on hand and foot by Han Shen's men, but the lord master himself, although polite and courteous, seemed to be in a thoughtful mood.

Christina, watching the two men, one so Occidental, and one so Oriental, found them both to be strong and masculine and rather formidable. She thought of her father, of his gentleness and understanding. She wondered whether the missionary, who was, according to Dr Kingsleigh, 'a jolly decent chap', was indeed her father's twin soul. I shall make him want to marry me, she thought, he must! I'll make myself into an indispensable wife. I'll wait on him hand and foot. I'll work like a dog at missionary chores. I'll even kowtow! He will be wonderful, I know he will! I am quite determined to become Paul Aubrey's wife.

Her face was sweet and innocent as she thought of perhaps having her own babies one day. She was so busy, living in a golden future of love, security and content, that she was unaware of two pairs of speculative, masculine eyes. As she day-dreamed by the thorn-fire, near the shelter made for Han Shen, Christina looked and felt beautiful. But despite her determination to marry Paul Aubrey, it was another face she saw before her, gleaming in the heart of the fire. She determinedly blinked it away.

Wang Ch'ung climbed the brow of the hill and then began to descend the other side. A swaggering raven squawked and flapped its wings as he walked by, then irritably resettled itself among the crabbed branches of a wild cherry tree. He ignored the bird, if, indeed, he saw it. He was engrossed in his thoughts—of the things discovered about the Sea Jade girl, and of his self-imposed task of finding the Aubrey Paul. He knew that the doctor and the fortune-teller, in their infinite wisdom, had decreed that it would be good joss to let the barbarian walk alone. This, so that the good nature spirits who lived in the hills could help him to find his soul. Wang Ch'ung, hearing what they had decided, felt the diagnosis to be wrong. He knew instinctively that Han Shen would never have agreed. He had indeed put the Christian in the doctor's and the wise man's hands, but the lord and master always had the final say. He was curious how this had happened as soon as Han Shen had gone—while he himself had also been away!

Wang Ch'ung had been busy, setting in motion the plans for discovering about the peasant girl. That had been the duty set for him, even though he would have preferred to go with his master, Szu-ma and the men. But he had gone about the task of meeting with friends and relations who could find out things, even in Peking. House of Han had been left in the major-domo's hands. The women and servants of the female part of the establishment were in the care of the dark old crow whom Wang Ch'ung despised. He found it in his heart to wish for Han Shen's speedy return. In the end, he had taken the initiative. There seemed to be nothing else to do but go after the despised barbarian. Was not auspicious to leave him out there alone!

Strictly speaking, the Aubrey Paul was none of the honourable Wang Ch'ung's business. The gods were being unkind. Fate was unspeakably disgusting. Such problems should not be placed even on the shoulders of a dog.

Dog! Repulsive, nauseous beast that had been nothing but trouble! Wang Ch'ung dwelt on thought of Rayn: that odious animal that had brought about the peasant girl's unnatural behaviour and concern. They had been so great that she had disobeyed instructions—which, in turn, brought her to the notice of Han Shen. What would the lord and master say when he learned the full truth? How would he react?

Wang Ch'ung hoped devoutly that he had acted wisely in the absence of his lord, whose instructions were being strictly carried out. Sea Jade was still, in the women's eyes, a lowly servant who had been brought in from

outside. He had taken it on himself to order that the dog
be allowed to stay with her. Even Wang Ch'ung believed
implicitly in the wise man's prediction of bad joss should
the animal be allowed to stay at the white man's side.
Now he was not so sure. The dog, who had rapidly
regained its strength, would have at least been some
protection for the half-witted wandering Englishman.

In a short time Wang Ch'ung reached a sheltered
place where there were ragged outcrops, and the
pointed breasts of hills nudged a molten-gold sky that
was already indigo far away in the east. Mottled shadows
had fallen to the ground like giant slabs of ink, and
night-flying hawks made swooping dart-like patterns in
the sky.

An old man sat immobile at the mouth of a cave. He
was at peace and alone. The skin was crinkled deeply
round his sickle-shaped eyes. His head was bald. He
wore the holy yellow robe. A begging-bowl and a
walking-staff had been placed at his side.

The old man made no sign of hearing Wang Ch'ung,
who stopped and kowtowed, in automatic respect for a
man who had devoted his life to the mystic Three-fold
Path. From the shoulder-bag he carried, Wang Ch'ung
put food in his bowl.

'I knew the Great One would send me a meal,' the
holy man said in a thin old voice. 'Go, and may God go
with you.'

'May you always have millet and rice,' Wang Ch'ung
replied politely. 'And blessings upon your head. Have
you seen a white man near here? He is ill and alone.'

'Seek and you will find,' the wise one said, and Wang
Ch'ung went on his way.

A full, round, glowing moon was making the sky silver
above the hills when Wang Ch'ung came to where Paul
Aubrey sat under a ledge of rock. The white man's hair
was clinging damply to a forehead glistening with sweat.
His thin pyjama-suit was clinging stickily to his long, thin
legs.

Aubrey continued to stare before him, paying no attention to the man who had appeared from the shadows. His eyes were wide open, and blank of expression. They did not flicker as Wang Ch'ung, in a rough, manly way, wiped his dusty face with a cloth. Then he sat down slowly and tucked his legs beneath him, to consider what it was best to do. Was the wise man right? Or should he follow his own instincts and get the barbarian back to the House of Han?

Perhaps the gods would give him the answer in their own good time. In a little while his hands searched inside his wide sleeves, and found Sea Jade's flute.

'The girl is not allowed any personal thing,' Han Shen had said. 'She is to be a nothing person, a nonentity —until I return.'

The flute was slim and fine, and its feel was smooth and gentle in his hands. Wang Ch'ung remembered his childhood, when the world had not been disgusting but a fine and wonderful place. He remembered his father and the little painted lady who had given him birth; he heard again the old music-teacher who had been too patient by far. It was all so far away. So long ago. He put the flute to his lips and began to play a tune from those far-away childhood days.

Aubrey's lips trembled. He turned his head slowly, half expecting to see a little Chinese princess with black waterfall hair. He was feeling in a confused way that this had happened before, but he could not remember. Thoughts came and went like will-o'-the-wisps in his mind, but always present was the killing pain.

Wang Ch'ung played for a long time, since the music kept him awake and on guard. The white man slept fitfully, waking always to agony, fighting to break through the barrier of red mist before his eyes, to regain control of reality. But, as before, everything slipped away.

The Hour of the Hare arrived. At five in the morning it was cold and unfriendly in the hills. Wang Ch'ung shook the man's sleeve, and then helped him up. That was the only assistance he received, and even through the web of agony, he sensed that the Chinaman did not like him. He wondered where the beautiful young girl had gone, and he felt an aching sense of loss, then a fresh wave of torment crashed through his brain and excluded all else.

Aubrey wondered if he had the strength to go on. Whether it mattered any more. Then he knew that it did, very much. And in the aching, throbbing torture of his mind he began to struggle again—to hold on to his life and on to his faith. But the world was receding in waves of red again. He groaned and stopped, then forced himself to walk on once more—after the man who was striding out so unfeelingly, just ahead . . .

Dawn tiptoed over the mountain tops and turned them to rose. The birds began to sing. Christina slept on until the sun streamed through the window and settled like warm gold silk on her face. She opened her eyes, blinking against the light. For a moment, she wondered where she was.

Then she remembered, and her lips quirked into a smile. She was at the magnificent home of Han Shen. She was under the same roof as her future husband! Oh yes, it must be! Marriage would solve all her problems, and—and what was more, she was fascinated by the idea. She felt excited, and warm and happy inside.

She jumped out of the carved bed and crossed the room to look out of the window. Her room was high up, giving her a good view, for she could see over the courtyard wall. The gardens were still and peaceful, typically Chinese. To the right, at the end of a paved pathway edged by trees and ornamental shrubs, were the outer gates, just visible from her vantage-point.

As she watched, the gatekeeper scrambled to his feet. His thin blue-cotton-clad figure bowed and scraped as he swung back the heavy wooden bar. Two people were coming through, and Christina's breath caught in her throat. The early light was gleaming on a man's fair hair. It was Paul Aubrey. It was! Her heart missed a beat.

He was tall and slim. As they drew nearer, she saw that Paul was staring before him, seeming to be unaware of his surroundings. Even at this distance she could see the lines of pain scored deeply across his forehead. His loose cotton tunic and trousers were creased and dirty. He looked desperately in need of love and care. He was younger than she had imagined, and more handsome by far! Her heart began to dance. Her cheeks glowed. Oh yes, it would be marvellous to be married to such a man!

There came a scratching at the door and a small girl entered with a tray bearing hot water, scented oil, hot flannels and a little butterfly-shape of soap.

'Good morning,' Dark Pebble said politely, and kowtowed.

'Good morning,' Christina replied.

Dark Pebble set the tray down on a black japanned table, and enquired, 'All ready now? Missee all ready for washy-wash?'

'Oh, that's quite all right,' Christina said hastily. 'I can wash myself.'

Dark Pebble, mystified, began to turn away, but Christina stopped her.

'Please don't go. Stay and talk to me. What is your name?'

'Dark Pebble.'

'How pretty!'

'Is beautiful when washed by glistening stream,' Dark Pebble agreed happily. 'Missee Sea Jade told me that. Missee Sea Jade like a loving *chiao-shih*—teacher, you say—to me.'

'I would like to meet your *chiao-shih*,' Christina said. 'She sounds nice.'

'Is beautiful and good. Allee same, in disgrace,' Dark Pebble went on sadly. 'She in lowly position, not like white lady who has been given finest, most important, room in ladies' house.'

'Why is Sea Jade in disgrace?'

'She defy lord and master. She walk with Ol'-Boy.'

'Ol' Boy?' Christina was mystified.

'He belong to missionary man.'

'Oh?' Christina was all ears now. 'Please tell me all about it, Dark Pebble. Ol' Boy—Is he a horse?'

'He big dog, all same with Missee Sea Jade now. Ol' Boy was going to get all finished, but he was saved by Missee Sea Jade. Missionary, he saved by her also. Allee same, she in trouble and disgrace.'

'Oh?' Christina felt confused. 'I am not sure I understand all this. Won't you please explain?'

When the morning wash ceremony had been completed and hot towels had soothingly covered Christina's face while she relaxed as instructed, she and Dark Pebble were deep in conversation. By the time breakfast had been brought in, and Christina had enjoyed millet cakes, pastry fingers, kumquats and weak, scented China tea, she had more or less learned the whole story. As she plied Dark Pebble with questions—and insisted on her sharing the delicious food—one thing came over loud and clear. Paul Aubrey owed his life to a young Chinese servant-girl. And the girl was devoted to his dog—and, Christina rather suspected, to the man himself.

'She sounds a kind person,' she told Dark Pebble, and genuinely meant it when she added, 'And I hope that she and I will become friends. When shall I meet her?'

'Night Bird, she say you go to tea-house at your convenience after morning meal. Sea Jade alone in Well of Happiness now.'

'Then we shall go to the Well of Happiness first.'

Dark Pebble gasped. 'Must not be! Night Bird, she say tea-house!'

Christina's brows rose high, then she smiled in a merry conspiratoral fashion. 'But we shall go to the women's courtyard first. I have made up my mind. I am not in disgrace, Dark Pebble, and I presume I am free to come and go as I choose? After all, I am a guest in this house.'

'Night Bird—she give orders!'

Christina's smile became frosty. 'Which is not very polite, don't you agree? One does not order guests about, and I believe it is one's duty to ignore bad manners in a hostess. Come along, take me to Sea Jade.'

Dark Pebble kowtowed, but there was a desperate look in her eyes. Night Bird hated, loathed and despised barbarians. Given her way, she would have them all burned alive. She was furious that the lord master had besmirched honourable House of Han by having them here. She was convinced that, by his actions, she and all under his roof were under sentence of death. Dark Pebble was in mortal terror of Night Bird, and sure that she would be lucky to live through the day by doing what she was about to do now.

'Will show honourable missee the way,' she said. 'Maybe Sea Jade all better now.'

She led Christina out of the house and into the courtyard, where Sea Jade was sitting under a tree, Rayn at her side. The dog wagged his tail at their approach and watched them with bright and enquiring eyes. Once the two young women were introduced, Dark Pebble scuttled away. With good joss on her side, the bright and pretty Beautiful Springtime and Summer Rain would have covered up her prolonged absence. They would, if they could. They were anxious to hear all about the white woman and to learn what she had to say.

Sea Jade looked at Christina, and thought her as strangely lovely as the kindly Fairweathers had been. She kowtowed, and there was infinite dignity and grace in the gesture.

Christina smiled, but did not hold out her hand. Touching in China was not considered to be polite; the usual thing was to put one's hands in one's sleeves and bow. Christina bowed her head, then looked down at Sea Jade and said warmly,

'I am very pleased to meet you. Dark Pebble tells me that you are just about the most perfect being on God's earth!'

'Little child responds to kind words,' Sea Jade replied. 'Hope gods be gentle to small person. One day, if possible, I will take her away from this place.'

'Oh?' Christina sat down on the ground beside Sea Jade, 'Then—if it is at all possible—I will help in any way I can.'

They were as one from that moment, their mutual desire to watch over and protect Dark Pebble giving them common ground on which to meet and talk. At once a warm feeling of liking and respect arose between them.

They were getting on like a house on fire when old Wang, firm and implacable, came to the Moon Gate, having sent a woman servant hurrying in.

'Will honourable white missee please join Madam Night Bird in Tea House of Midday Sun. Will Chinee girl go at once to great lord's presence. Is wise to go quickly. Go chop chop!'

The two girls looked over to where Wang stood watching them.

'Goodbye,' Sea Jade breathed, wanting to die. So the Lord Han Shen had returned!

'Until later,' Christina said firmly.

Sea Jade fled, wondering just how bad her punishment would be.

She and Rayn followed Wang through to the men's part of the house and to the lord master's study. Han Shen was sitting at his desk, his arms folded in his sleeves, a supercilious look in his eyes. She lowered her own gaze to the floor.

'I hear that your disobedience grows rather than lessens,' he said. 'That shows complete lack of grace.'

She looked up at that, and even though her heart was

racing, she was defying him with her eyes.

'Forgive, please,' she said in her clear, lovely voice. 'Is unforgivable to lose grace. Even worse—to lose face! I made solemn oath to barbarian. I look after dog.'

'And if I tell you that all that is unnecessary now?'

'Is necessary—until barbarian say everything all right.'

'What if I command you to let the dog go?'

It was no peasant looking at him now, but the noble, deliciously lovely Miss Ling Sea Jade.

'August lord,' she said quietly. 'Even Madam Night Bird's cane could not sway me from doing my duty. Ol' Boy and I must be as one spirit—until the Englishman, he says, all finish and done.'

He heard no more than 'Madam Night Bird's cane'. Anger was making a cold knot inside him, yet why, he could not fathom. He had himself thought the girl deserving of a whipping only moments before. Now furious, he decided to reprimand Number One Woman severely. Night Bird was in high position simply because she had outlived most of his father's first concubines and wives, and he had often wished that he could rid himself of her—and some of the others, too. The young ones, who had been mere children when his aged father had taken them on, were no problem at all, but Night Bird! His anger grew.

He looked at Sea Jade, who was holding Rayn's collar, and said coldly, 'You may keep the dog. You will also see to it that you are ready to serve the white people at all times. This because you are able to understand their tongue. You will answer to me rather than to Number One Lady. Even so, you will be obedient and honourable in action, as tradition demands. Do I make myself clear?'

'Yes, lord.'

'You will work hard and fill your days with dutiful thoughts. You have caused me great trouble and displeasure. You are unworthy.'